Prologue -

She could see the flaming torches t smoke of fires burning in the still night. They were n eaving their way through the thick undergrowth, gradually drawing The villagers would have had to travel through fields and hedgerows, climbing hills and crossing streams for many miles to reach the château. It was dark and warm and Sophie could see the stars very distinctly in the night sky. In the distance, she could hear the shouts of the men and women, angry tones juxtaposed against the clear, sultry night.

Her heart was beating faster as they drew closer. She had to try to keep calm and think sensibly; everyone had left the château at dawn. The Comte, Comtesse, and their three young children had fled along the graveled drive in a carriage, hoping to get to the safety of England. They had friends across the sea, who had agreed to take them in as soon as they had heard about what was happening in France.

Since the king had been executed, nobody of noble birth in France was safe. As soon as they could, the family had escaped. Sophie had been left behind; she was sure the Comtesse must have forgotten about her in the rush to get away and would send someone back for her. As the day had lengthened, Sophie realised she had to fight for herself, as there was no one left to help her. She looked around the empty room and her eyes fell upon the portrait of the family dressed in fine, rich silks: the beautiful Comtesse, her jewels sparkling in the firelight and drinking chocolate from an engraved, silver pot. It occurred to Sophie that she meant no more to the family than any of their possessions, even though she was family and governess to their children.

Oh, how she missed the children! The eldest, Colette, at twelve years old was growing into a wonderfully accomplished young woman, who could have been Sophie's sister they looked so alike. The eight-year-old twins, Luc and Yves, were extremely lively young boys and, despite always getting into trouble, she wished they were here now. She would have forgiven them any misdemeanours. As for the rest of the servants, they had deserted their posts days ago, but as a governess to the children, Sophie was in a difficult position: her proper station in life was halfway between servant and family.

Now, with the revolutionary mob approaching, Sophie knew she needed to escape but she was terrified as to where to go. Was it time to run or hide? She looked out of the window again: they were almost through the woods. Soon they would begin the long walk along the avenue of trees. She really must get moving if she was going to have the chance to escape. The angry horde would not spare her or the house.

All over France there had been murder, looting, and destroyed property because of the revolution. Her cousin, the Comtesse, had left with nothing but her children and husband. They had taken no possessions with them on their journey, the need to escape was so great.

Sophie could not believe they had left without her and felt quite let down, especially by her cousin. She sat for a few minutes contemplating what to do. Maybe she had done something wrong and that was why her cousin had left her behind. Sophie was becoming desperate. She looked up at the portrait again and the jewels in the painting caught her eye. Then she remembered that the family jewels were still in the house. If she could save them for the Comtesse, at least that would be something to bring her back into the family fold.

    She leaped up, grabbed a candlestick from the mantelpiece, and ran along the corridor out into the hallway and up the spiral staircase to the Comtesse's chambre, where she knew the jewels were hidden. Sophie ran along the upper corridor until she reached the Comtesse's door. She put her hand on the doorknob and turned it - thank God it wasn't locked! Sophie entered the darkroom and ran across to a large, polished, wooden casket. On top was a small wooden chest, heavily engraved with fruit and flowers. She knew this was where the Comtesse kept her jewellery. Sophie went straight to it and tried to open it, but, of course, it was locked. She stood still, breathing heavily, her hand on her forehead.

    'Think Sophie, think,' she said to herself, and then she remembered. She turned around and ran over to the Comtesse's bedside and slid her hand under the mattress, as she had seen her cousin do many times before. Luckily, the key was there, tucked safely away under the mattress. Her heart was beating very fast; she had beads of sweat on her upper lip; and, as she reached out to put the key into the lock of the small chest, her hands were shaking. Sophie gripped her right wrist with her left hand to steady it. She tried not to panic as she slid the key into the lock of the chest. With a loud click, the lock sprang open. Swiftly, she opened the two small doors on the front of the chest: inside there were two small top drawers set side by side with four bigger drawers underneath. She took out the top two drawers and looked around for something to put the jewellery into. There was nothing suitable, so Sophie removed her silk shawl from her shoulders and laid it out on the floor. In the candlelight, the jewels sparkled magnificently. There was no time to stare in admiration at the wonderful rubies, emeralds, diamonds, and gold. She tipped drawer after drawer onto the shawl. One by one, she emptied the contents of the drawers until the chest stood empty. The drawers were scattered all over the floor in her haste. When she had finished, she gathered up the corners of the shawl and looked around the room to find something to tie up her precious pile. On the dressing table she saw some neatly coiled ribbons; quickly, she pulled one out and used it to tie up the shawl.

    By this time, she could hear the shouts and cries of the people approaching. A quick glance out of the window and she could see they were already halfway down the drive. She knew she had to move very fast to get away. Gathering her skirt up over her bundle of jewellery and holding it in one hand and the candlestick in the other, Sophie ran down the corridor to the back stairs, which would take her straight to the kitchen. As she ran down the stairs, her head was whirling about what she was going to do. She tried to think clearly but her heart was still pounding and she trembled all over. Sophie stood in the kitchen and she put the candlestick down on the large, pine, scrubbed table. The candle had burnt down very low and she decided to take a new one from the wooden candle box on the kitchen dresser. She quickly pulled the old candle out of the stick and used it to light the new one. The kitchen was at the back of the house and the mob was at the front. She knew all the doors were locked, but that would not keep them out for long. She must think of some way to escape. If only there was someone to turn to, but everyone had left. Sophie glanced around the room, taking in the massive fireplace where Agnes the cook made all the meals, the copper pans shining in the candlelight. High up along one wall was a rack of metal hooks; all the keys to the house and outbuildings were kept on this rack. Maybe she could hide in one of the barns, but surely the mob would search them and maybe even set fire to them.

Then she remembered somewhere that would make an excellent hiding place: buried in the grounds of the château was an ice house. It was brick-built with several chambers and it was used to store ice for use in the kitchen. As it was summer, it would not be completely full of ice. She knew it was connected to the house by a tunnel that was accessed from the cellar. If she could make it to the ice house, maybe she could hide there until the angry horde dispersed. The door to the tunnel was in the cellar under the main kitchen. She ran to a small, painted, wooden door in the corner. The handle turned easily and, as the door opened, it revealed a stone, spiral staircase. Grabbing the candlestick, she stepped in through the door, carefully closing it behind her as she did so. She suddenly felt the air around her get much colder. The tunnel was dark and she could just see in the dim light given off by the candle that the curved ceiling and walls were green with algae and dripping with water. If she could get to the ice house, maybe there would be a chance to get away. As Sophie descended the stone steps, the air became quite musty and damp smelling.

Sophie practically threw herself down the stone steps, hoping she could remember the way through the cellars and find the tunnel to the ice house. The cellars were vast. As well as wine, all manner of things were stored in the various rooms. She held the candle up in front of her to help light the way: cobwebs were everywhere! This was no time to be scared of spiders, but she shuddered as a cobweb brushed across her cheek. Sophie thought the entrance to the tunnel was at the west end of the cellar. At the bottom of the steps she needed to turn left and make her way through the walls lined with shelves, containing jars of bottled fruit, crates of apples, large stone jars of cider and barrels of beer. Sophie was starting to feel tired, but she knew she had to press on.

She was under the courtyard now. The throng of people had no idea she was there, literally under their feet. As she was nearing the ice house, they were breaking into the château.

Above her on the drive, the angry crowd had entered the courtyard at the front of the château. There were dozens of them stretched out across the front of the château; many of them were carrying pitchforks and axes. There was the sound of breaking glass, as they smashed their way into the main hallway. The angry mob scattered; some of them wanted to torch the place.

'Burn it to the ground!' someone cried.
'No, take what you want and smash the rest.'

'To the cellars!' shouted another man. 'The Comte has a wonderful wine cellar – let's take the wine.'

And with that, the crowd turned and all tried to push their way down the stone steps to the cellar.

The thought of hiding in a freezing cold ice house was not something Sophie was too happy about, as she knew, apart from being extremely cold and damp, it would be full of spiders and possibly rats. 'But,' she concluded, 'the ice house might save my life.'

Chapter One.

'Oh great!' The lift was broken again. That meant four flights of stairs and Roselinde was not in the mood for struggling up the cold, dark stairway after the day she had been through. Let's face it, not just the day, but the week, month and even the year were all going to pot.

It had been raining all afternoon and Ros was saturated. Her hair was plastered to her face and she'd realised her shoes had been leaking badly, making it difficult to walk. She couldn't put her hand up to her face to wipe away the stream of water that was running down it, because she had two huge carrier bags bulging with groceries.

As she trudged up the stairs, Ros thought, 'there must be more to life than this!' Her latest photographic assignment for *House Today* magazine had been an unmitigated disaster. She could not find the address that her editor had emailed her and when she finally arrived, the middle-aged couple, whose home she was supposed to be photographing, were having a blazing row and they decided that she would make an excellent referee. It was an extremely uncomfortable situation that she would have rather avoided.

Rosalinde reached her front door and set down the bags on the mat, wiped her face with her scarf, and delved into her coat pocket for the key. She pushed the key into the lock and shoved the heavy door open. Jake, her beautiful, black cat, was curled up on the old, worn sofa. He lifted his head up and looked at her in contempt, his eyes saying, 'where on earth have you been?'

'Ok, Jake, I know it's way past your dinner time. Just let me get in and I'll feed you, Your Majesty.'

Jake jumped off the sofa, stretched and walked over to where Ros had dumped the shopping bags on the floor. Sniffing the air, he stuck his nose into the bag containing a packet of fresh prawns.

'Get out of there now, young man!' shouted Rosalinde. 'They're not for you!'

Quickly, she picked up the bags and placed them on the kitchen worktop.

'Right, I'll feed you first. Then I can get on without you under my feet.' Jake was now winding himself in and out of her legs. She opened the slim kitchen cupboard and reached up to the top shelf – it was the only place the cat biscuits were safely out of his reach! Too many times she had returned from work and found empty cat food boxes, ripped to shreds on the kitchen floor. Rosalinde bent down to pick up Jake's bowl, rinsed it under the tap, gave it a wipe, and filled it with salmon flavored biscuits. He was purring loudly now, jumping up on his back legs, eager to get at the bowl of food.

'There you go,' she said, as she placed the bowl on the floor. He immediately stuck his face in the bowl and started crunching up the biscuits.

A cool glass of white wine was what she needed. She reached to open the fridge door and was interrupted by the phone ringing. 'Great!' she thought to herself.

'Hello?'

'Hello, Rosalinde, it's Janet. How was your day?' Janet was her editor at the magazine.

'Um...well, actually it was bloody awful! They were a dreadful pair and...'

'Yes, but did you get the pics?' As usual, Janet was not interested in details, just the bottom line, which was whether or not she had the pictures for her magazine.

'Yes. It looks like the pictures will be great. It was a gorgeous house – just a shame about the owners."

'Good – excellent – well done! Now, how do you feel about a trip to France?' Janet, as usual, got straight to the point.

'I'm interested...tell me more.' Rosalinde wasn't really listening; she was thinking about the lovely, chilled bottle of Sauvignon Blanc waiting for her in the fridge and she was desperate to get Janet off the phone, so she could pour herself a large glass and then soak in the bath with her book and wine.

'I want September's issue to be a special on a French château. I've got a long list of château owners, who are very keen to have their homes in the magazine, and some that are not so keen, but that I think would be far more interesting. I will sift through the pile and narrow it down to two or three.'

Janet was on a roll and when she was like this, there was no stopping her. Rosalinde decided to agree with everything she said; she knew from experience it was the easiest way to get her off the phone. She could phone her back in a day or two to get more details.

'Ok, Janet, that sounds like my sort of thing. I'll be in touch soon. I must go, as my pasta is boiling dry,' she lied.

With that, Ros hung up. The guilt she felt about telling a little white lie regarding the pasta lasted about thirty seconds. Then she opened the fridge door and reached in for the chilled bottle of wine. She pulled the cork and poured herself a large glassful. The first cool mouthful immediately hit the spot; Rosalinde could feel it going all the way down. She stood leaning up against the worktop in the tiny, warm kitchen savoring the crisp, fresh taste. Before she had realised it, she had drained the glass. Her mind was all over the place lately and she was finding it very difficult to concentrate on anything. She poured a second glass and carried it through to the bathroom, setting it on the side of the bath. She bent down to put the plug in and then turned on the taps. She poured in some bubble bath and, leaving the bath to fill, went into the bedroom to undress. As Ros lay in the bath, her mind drifted to everything and nothing. Perhaps a trip to France would help to sort her mind out and give her a chance to make a fresh start. She started to relax and unwind.

Later on, after her bath, she was feeling much better: clean, fresh, warm, and the two glasses of wine had contributed to her lovely rosy glow. Rosalinde had time to think about what Janet had said to her on the phone about the trip to France. Ros decided she quite liked the idea of a trip away – it was just what she needed, right at this moment. Her life was completely stuck in a rut and she felt as if she was going nowhere.

Rosalinde had recently split up from her long-term boyfriend, Matt. They had drifted apart because of their various work commitments. Although they had been together for two years, their families adored each other and, of course, everyone expected them to settle down and get married, they just couldn't seem to make it work. 'Ahh, Matt, we had some great times together,' she thought. They had been away on holiday last year to Greece and it was wonderful; they had both totally relaxed. She had thought he was going to propose, but it never happened and, when they returned, things started to fall apart. Rosalinde's mother was convinced they would get back together, as was Matt's, but Ros and Matt knew it was over, even though they both still had some feelings for each other. Some days she missed him so much it hurt, but then she remembered the rows and felt relieved it was over. In any case, he had moved to Scotland and they moved in different circles now.

Rosalinde decided tomorrow she would ring Janet and find out more about the assignment in France. She would have to brush up on her schoolgirl French. Yes, why not? She was ready for an adventure in France, a change of scenery and all that French wine and lovely French food. She'd always loved French food, especially mussels, oysters and crusty bread – she could already taste it. 'Yummy!' She thought and began to feel quite excited.

'Right, Jake, off to bed! I've got a busy day tomorrow.' And with that, she switched off the lights and turned in for the night.

Chapter Two.

Guy was fed up. Life was always so hard, he thought. Why couldn't he have been born rich? He had never had enough money to do the kind of things he wanted to do. Most of his friends were content to drift along with their ordinary, banal lives, going to their mundane jobs with basic incomes, but he wanted more than that and he was determined that was exactly what he was going to achieve – legally, or not.

He had moved from Rennes, in Brittany, to the busy market town of Avranches, in Normandy. His family had disowned him years ago. He had never toed the line, always in trouble as a teenager. As he grew older, they had tired from bailing him out of trouble. Now approaching middle age, he had not lost any of his arrogance. Guy thought that moving to a smaller town would give him some advantages. In his head, he thought he would somehow become a bigger person in the community and, therefore, more important. Sadly, this was totally untrue. To himself, he was charming, gracious, and extremely generous, but most people thought him to be a lazy, ignorant bully.

Guy walked into Sebastian's bar on Monday at 12 p.m. precisely. Usually in France everyone stopped for lunch; most people had a two and a half-hour lunch break and nearly all the French took their main meal of the day at this time. The café bar was packed. He wove his way through the busy tables, until he found a table situated at the back of the café in a dark corner. It would suit him just fine. Sebastian's was not the smartest bar in the town – it was a bit sad looking. The peach coloured wallpaper was peeling off in one or two corners and the floor had quite a few scuff marks and chips in the old-fashioned Lino, which covered it. Guy sank back into the worn, red, leatherette upholstery and looked around the room: there was the usual bunch of office workers, a few farmers, and some British and Belgian tourists. He couldn't see anyone he knew, so he settled down to wait for Vivienne, Sebastian's wife, to come over and take his order. Guy glanced through the menu and when Vivienne came over to his table to take his order, he had made his choice.

'Bonjour, monsieur. Have you chosen what you would like?' she asked.
'Oui. I will have a Niçoise salad and a small carafe of your house white wine.'
Vivienne thanked him for his order and swiftly walked away to the kitchen. As she walked away, Guy watched her weave her way through the tables and thought what a lucky man Sebastian was. Vivienne was a beautiful, vivacious woman with
long, thick, dark, curly hair and piercing, light blue eyes. She was neatly dressed and had an amazing figure and, to top it off, she always wore very sexy high heeled shoes. Guy had noticed that today she was wearing a tight white shirt, black pencil skirt, and bright red stilettos, which matched her lipstick perfectly.

He sat back in his seat and looked around him at the other diners. They were all talking animatedly to their respective partners and not really taking any notice of him staring at them. There were the usual conversations about families and friends; the farmers were talking about the weather and stock prices; then he noticed a young couple gazing into each other's eyes, who were completely oblivious to the noise and movement going on around them. He felt quite jealous looking at them, so he pulled a face and turned his head away from them. In the opposite corner, he spotted an altogether different couple. Guy had never seen them in Sebastian's before. It was obvious that they were not tourists, because of the way they were dressed and their local accents.

They were two middle-aged men, both quite scruffy and very dubious looking. Guy, being nosy, tuned his hearing into their conversation. What he heard made his ears prick up immediately, as it was extremely interesting.

'I'm telling you, that old woman is sitting on a fortune,' said the first man.

'Rubbish! It's no longer there – the Nazis found it in 1942,' replied the second man.

'No, they could not find it. It's still at the château, Henri!' said Michel. 'Diamonds, emeralds and rubies.'

'I don't believe you, Michel. I have seen Madame La Roche – she is as poor as a church mouse.'

'Ah, that is because she does not know about the jewels.'

'Well, where are they then, Michel? How do you know that they actually exist?'

'They are in the château – I have already told you that – but as for their exact location, I'm not so sure.'

Henri ran his hand over his stubbly chin, deep in thought. He wondered if they could find the jewels and what they would be worth.

At the same moment, Guy was thinking exactly the same thing, but he needed to know – no, he was desperate to know – more, like where was the château and how could he get his hands on the valuables? Should he approach these two reprobates, or should he try to find out the information for himself? He was so self-absorbed that when Vivienne brought his lunch to the table, she had to ask him three times to move his hands from the placemat, so she could set down his plate. Even with a delicious Niçoise salad placed in front of him, he still just sat staring into space. His mind was racing. 'If only I could find this place and get my hands on the jewels, I would be rich for life, but can I do it on my own?' He looked up and realised Sebastian was staring at him, because he hadn't touched his food or wine. Guy smiled at Sebastian and quickly unwrapped his knife and fork from the napkin and began eating his salad. 'They must be wondering what's wrong with me,' he thought, as he tucked in. The salad was excellent as always, with just the right amount of lovely oil and vinegar dressing, and the wine was lovely, dry and cool, just how he liked it.

As he ate, he watched the two men and he decided to follow them when they left the café. If he could find these jewels, he'd be rich – be set for life – he wouldn't have to work ever again. He fantasized about how it would be, to be so rich.

Henri and Michel were still discussing the château and how they would like to find the jewels for themselves.

'Henri, I think we should take a trip over to the château and offer our services to the widow LaRoche.'

'What do you mean?' asked Henri.

'Well, we could pretend to be odd job men and say we could mend her roof or sort out the plumbing and, whilst we are there, we can be looking for the jewels.'

'Oh yes, I see what you are talking about, but won't she be suspicious?'

'We must make ourselves presentable, or she will not employ us, and whatever happens, you must not mention the jewels in front of her.'

'I am not a fool, Michel – do not treat me as such!' exclaimed Henri. He was not an idiot and resented the fact that Michel treated him as one.

'Ok, I am sorry, but we must be careful. The slightest slip and we will be found out and our plans will be ruined. Right, let's go. I am keen to get over there and have a look at the place.'

Guy looked up and he realised the two men were leaving the café. He quickly dropped a twenty euro note on the table, which was considerably more than his lunch had cost, but he didn't have time to wait for change; he had to follow the two men. He got up and followed them out of the door. He started to panic, in case he lost them.

Henri and Michel wandered up the road. People were on their way back to work and the traffic was heavy through the centre of town. They had to pause at a small roundabout, because there was so much traffic trying to negotiate the one-way system.

Henri and Michel walked up a narrow side road away from the town centre and stopped outside a shabby, brown door. Henri took the key from his pocket and slid it into the lock. He opened the door and the two of them went inside. Guy was standing on the corner, watching them. Once they were safely inside, he decided to go and get his car; then he would go to the nearest shop to buy some cigarettes and a newspaper. He walked quickly back to the car, jumped in and set off. Luckily, the traffic had calmed down, so he managed to get back to the narrow side street fairly quickly. There was a Tabac shop across the road on the corner, so he ran in there, grabbed a newspaper, and asked for twenty cigarettes. He paid, gestured thank you, and walked out of the shop. Guy went back to his car and he could see the rundown apartment that the two men had just entered from the front seat. It had taken him half an hour to get back and settle in the car. He lit a cigarette and sat back. He could see that the lights were on inside the apartment; they cast shadows of the two men moving about inside.

His mind was racing. What if there really was something of value in this château that the two old men were on about? How was he going to find out where it was? And how on earth would he get his hands on it?

The air inside the car was thick with smoke and Guy was becoming increasingly impatient. The two old men had been inside for three hours. He was beginning to think it wasn't worth the effort when, finally, the lights went off and a few seconds later the door opened. Guy was instantly alert; he sat up in his seat and switched on the engine.

Henri and Michel had changed into clean clothes that weren't nearly so shabby as their previous attire and had washed and combed their hair. They walked down the road and got into an old, faded, blue Renault van. As they drove off, Guy pulled out into the traffic behind them, keeping fairly well back so they would not get suspicious, although he was fairly certain they had no idea he even existed.

As they drove out of the town, the traffic became less and soon they were on a very quiet main road leading to Mont St. Michel. Guy kept well back. As the road was completely straight and there was nowhere to hide, he tried to drive with a few cars in between himself and the blue Renault van. They drove on into the town of Pontorson. When they reached the mini roundabout on the edge of the town, they turned left over the railway crossing. Guy wondered where the hell they were going, as they left the town behind them. They were out in the open countryside now. All the trees were budding up and the bocage at the side of the road was covered with primroses. Spring was definitely in the air, thought Guy, as they drove along. All the while, the roads were becoming narrower and more winding. He was having to be more careful now, so that they did not realise he was following them.

He rounded a sharp bend in the road and there in front of him, through a gap in the trees, was the most fantastic château he had ever seen. He could just make out the size and shape of it through the leaves of the trees. The blue van had driven further on and he could see it had turned into the long, tree-lined, gravel driveway.

Guy stopped the car and got out. The sight before him was stunning: the château was built in some sort of pink tinged stone and, as the sunlight fell on it, it glowed.

It had beautiful, grey slates on the turreted roof that shone in the afternoon sun. He could see that the garden was well kept, the lawns neatly cut, and the walls of the château were surrounded by hydrangeas, which would soon be flowering. He could imagine them all out in flower in various shades of pink and blue, as there were so many like them around the area.

The blue van had disappeared, and he guessed it had driven round to the back of the main building. He could just hear the engine cease and the two van doors open and slam shut. Guy realised he was too far away to hear any conversations that the two old men might have, either between themselves or with the inhabitants of the château.

Michel walked up to the back door of the château and pulled the black, cast iron bell pull. He and Henri had decided, as they were acting as tradesmen, they should use the back entrance.

'Henri, stand still! Stop shuffling about and put your cap on straight.'

'Ok, ok. I'm just a bit nervous, Michel. I'll be alright in a minute,' said Henri.

They stood at the old, wooden door for a few minutes before they could hear footsteps coming towards them from inside. Finally, the old door creaked open to reveal an elderly man, dressed in grey trousers and a dark blue blazer. He looked very weary and his hands were badly crippled with arthritis.

'Oui?' barked Didier, the elderly butler.

'Bonjour, monsieur,' said Michel, taking a deep breath. 'My friend and I were wondering if you had any odd jobs you wanted doing around the place. We can turn our hand to most jobs, such as painting, woodwork, cleaning gutters out. Any job inside or outside.'

'Um,' thought Didier. What should he do? There were loads of jobs that needed to be done around the house and, God knew he had tried, but his old hands were becoming useless. The problem was that he knew his mistress, Madame La Roche, who owned the château – and the estate for that matter – was very short of money.

'How much would you charge per hour, for example?' he asked them.

'Well, it depends on the job, but I should think twenty euros an hour for the two of us, plus materials of course,' said Michel.

Didier thought that sounded extremely cheap and wondered what the catch was, but he was really rather desperate for some extra help around the place, so he decided to engage them on a simple task to see how well they could work and to see if they were reliable.

'Ok, Monsieurs, come back tomorrow at 9 o'clock and I will give you some work for the day. We will see how you get on.'

'Merci, Monsieur. We will not let you down. See you tomorrow.'

Didier closed the door and walked back along the dark hall. Now all he had to do was convince Madame that engaging the two men was a good idea. He knocked on the salon door and quietly entered the room. Mathilde La Roche was sitting in an old, worn armchair facing the fireplace, reading a newspaper.

'Bonsoir, Madame.'

'Bonsoir, Didier,' she said, looking up from her paper. 'Did I hear someone at the door?'

'Oui, Madame. It was two local men looking for work.' Here we go, he thought – I will just have to come out with it.

'I took the liberty of asking them to return tomorrow, as there are several jobs that need attention and, as you know, Madame, I cannot manage the heavy work anymore.'

'Very well, Didier. I think that's a very good idea.' Mathilde knew the château was in dire need of an upgrade, but funds were running very low. She was typical of many château owners: asset rich, but cash poor. 'I have received another letter from the English magazine, who wrote to me a while ago. They are coming to interview me and to photograph the château inside and out. They will be here on the fifteenth of June, in about two weeks' time, so it will be good to get the place tidied up a bit.'

'Oui, Madame,' Didier replied, thinking to himself that it meant a lot more work for him. He sighed heavily and let himself out of the room.

Although Mathilde was not at all keen to take part in this magazine nonsense, she was well aware it would bring in some much-needed income. As an elderly woman on her own, she was in a very vulnerable position. Her only son had died some years ago and, at eighty-five, she knew her life was ebbing away. She did not want to sell the château and was becoming increasingly concerned as to what she should do to secure its future. To sell up was the easy option, but somehow, she just couldn't. Her husband's ancestors had owned the château for over three hundred years, and she was not going to be the one who sold up and broke the linage. The time was coming for decisions to be made, but not today.

Guy was still hanging around outside, wondering what to do. He realised he needed more information about the château before he could either break in and look for the treasure, or take a more subtle approach and try and con his way in. He decided to call it a day and go home. His girlfriend, Therese, would be home from the hair salon where she worked by now. She knew loads of gossip about the locals – surely, she would know something useful. As he drove home, he mulled over the day's events. Maybe this was the opportunity he was searching for. It wasn't going to be easy and he didn't want Therese to suspect anything, so he must try to keep calm.

Guy slid his key into the lock and entered the apartment he shared with Therese. 'Hi,' he called, as he walked through the door.

'Bonsoir, chérie. Have you had a good day?' Therese replied from the kitchen.

'Yes, quite interesting actually. Pour me a drink and I will tell you all about it.'

Therese took two small glasses from the old, wooden cabinet and poured them both a Pastis and then added some water to the glasses. She carried the two small glasses through to their tiny sitting room and sat beside him on the old, worn sofa. 'So, what have you been up to today?' she asked, hoping he was going to say he had been looking for work or had actually found a job.

'Therese, what do you know about the pink château just outside of Pontorson?'

'Why?' she asked.

'I'm just interested, that's all.'

Therese sat back and sighed. 'Here we go again,' she thought. 'Another hair-brained scheme.' She was beginning to see that she had made a mistake letting Guy move in with her. He was lazy and, she suspected, not always on the right side of the law. 'Well, Madame Mathilde La Roche owns it and it has been in the family for years and years.' She paused to take a sip of her drink and light a cigarette. 'The Gestapo had it as their headquarters during the war.'

Guy's ears pricked up at this piece of information. His mind began to race, as the Gestapo and the Nazis were notorious for stealing anything of value. What if there were jewels or gold hidden in the house? One of the old men thought they were still there, that the Nazis had not found anything during the war.

'Guy, why are you interested in the château? I didn't know that you knew it even existed.'

'Well, I drove past it and thought it looked quite an interesting house. Although it is quite run down, so I thought I might ask if they had any work they needed doing,' he lied.

'Um, they say the widow LaRoche is penniless – I wouldn't bother if I was you. Why don't you get yourself a proper job? You are not stupid – I am sure you could get a good job. Shall I ask around and see if there is anything going locally?'

Guy was just about to shout at her and tell her what he thought of the job idea and then he thought better of it. If she thought he was looking for a job, it would keep her happy and it would divert her attention away from his plans at the château. 'Yes, ok then, see what you can find.'

'Right, I'll start tomorrow. I will ask my brother, Ralph, if he knows of anything. Now, what would you like for supper?'

'Have you got any steak?'

'Yes, ok. Steak and salad. You open a bottle of wine and I will start cooking.'

'Good,' thought Guy, 'she has forgotten about the château already.' He walked into the tiny kitchen and pulled a bottle of red wine from the rack. He wiped his hand over the label to remove the dust: it was a bottle of Burgundy. 'Lovely,' he thought, 'that will go well with steak.' Guy opened the wine and poured a small amount into a glass. He sipped it. It was warm and rich, so he filled the two glasses on the worktop and handed one to Therese, who was making a salad. Everything was calm and he was acting as normally as he possibly could, but inside his head kept drifting back to the château. He must remain calm, he told himself, and not raise Therese's suspicions.

'Put some music on, chérie,' she said.

'Ok.' Good – they were both relaxing. He felt sure she was not suspicious about the château Guy went back into the sitting room and selected an Edith Piaf CD. He slid it into the CD player and turned up the volume. He plonked himself down in his favorite, comfy armchair and closed his eyes. He was feeling more relaxed. He reached over and picked up the glass of wine from the coffee table, taking a large swig, as his mind wandered back to the château – he was obsessed! He needed to think of a way in, an excuse to look around. If he could get in with the old woman, maybe he could have a good snoop around.

He had spent most of the night tossing and turning and the following morning he had a terrible headache – too much red wine, he decided. 'Pull yourself together,' he told himself. He was going to call on Madame La Roche and offer his services as a painter and decorator. Hopefully, she would take him on, and he would gain access to all the rooms in the château. He was feeling pretty clever.

He kissed Therese goodbye and set off for the château. It was a lovely sunny morning; the air was clear with just a little bit of mist sitting in the shallow valleys. As he drove along, his mind was working overtime. How was he going to convince the old woman to let him work at the château? He had to admit, he didn't look much like a painter and decorator. Stupidly, he had worn a smart jacket, shirt, and trousers.

As he drew up to the château, he saw the two old men that he had seen the day before unloading tools and ladders from their old van.

'Oh no!' he blurted out. 'They have beaten me to it.' *Bang!* He hit the steering wheel with his fists in frustration. What the hell was he going to do now? There was no way the old woman was going to hire another painter and decorator. He would have to think of something else. He turned the car around and sped off up the road. All the fire had gone out of him and he was feeling very despondent; his mind was in a fog and he could not think of anything other than getting into that house.

Beep, beep! A horn roared in his ear, which woke him up just in time. He nearly ran into a car coming from the other direction. The driver passed by, shaking his fist and gesturing rudely at him. He was furious, but knew he must calm down. Guy decided to go into Pontorson to a bar – he needed a drink! He would clear his head and think up another way to get access to the château.

Chapter Three.

'Hi, Mum. How are you?' asked Rosalinde.

'Oh, not so bad, darling. What are you up to at the moment? I haven't seen you for ages!' replied Ellen.

'Well, I've got a great new assignment in France. I'm off to Normandy at the end of the week. I'm going to photograph two châteaux for the magazine that I work for. It's for a special French edition.'

'Lovely,' said Ellen, but her heart began racing and her mouth became very dry.

She knew the time that she had put off for years had come. She could no longer pretend that Rosalinde would not find out about the past and she knew Rosalinde had a right to know about her background. Ellen knew she should have been straight with Ros years ago, but she was a coward. Maybe she could get away with not telling her anything for a bit longer – after all, Normandy was a big place. The chance of her actually coming face to face with anyone connected to her was pretty remote.

'Look, love, why don't you come round before you go to France? There are a few things I would like to go over with you.'

'I'd love to, Mum. I'll see if I have any time tomorrow. Anyway, I must go – lots to do.'

And with that, Rosalinde rang off. Ellen was left staring at the phone in her hand with a massive feeling of dread, starting in her chest and then spreading all over her. She must see Rosalinde and tell her the truth. Ros was a sensible girl. Ellen hoped she would take what she had to tell her in her stride and not get upset or blame her for not telling her sooner.

Before she had realised, it was Friday and Rosalinde had not been to see Ellen. She was booked on the overnight ferry from Portsmouth to Saint-Malo. As she sat in the queue, waiting to board the ferry in her car, Ros remembered her mother had wanted to talk to her, so she decided to give her a ring. She pulled her mobile from her bag and dialed the number. After a few rings, her mother's answer machine picked up the phone.

'Hello, this is Ellen Wilson. I am sorry I cannot get to the phone right now. Please leave a message after the tone.'

'Hello, Mum. Sorry I didn't get back to you – it's been rather hectic this week. I'm going to be away for about ten days or so, but I'll ring you in a couple of days to let you know how I'm getting on. Love you. Bye.'

As soon as she hung up, she realised the queue had begun to move forward and soon her car was travelling up the ramp and onto the very large ferry. Travelling on the ferry was a new experience for Rosalinde; usually she flew everywhere, but she had decided to take her own car, as she would be covering quite a few miles whilst in France and she had heard that the roads were very good. She parked on the car deck and turned off her engine. As she did, a French stewardess knocked on her car window.

'Bonjour, Madame.'

'Bonjour,' said Rosalinde a little nervously, and the stewardess handed her a small piece of card.

'This is your door number. Remember it for when we dock in the morning – it will make it easier to find your car.'

'Merci,' said Ros.

She looked at the card and it said D6. Up ahead of her, she could see a doorway with people going through it; above it, it said D6. 'Ok,' she thought to herself, 'I'd better get going.' She pulled her night bag out of the boot of the car, making sure her camera and other equipment were safely locked away, and made her way through the cars, vans and trailers to D6. Two flights of stairs stood between her and the information desk. She showed them her ticket and they gave her a key card for her cabin. She was on the right deck for the cabin; she just had to find out which side of the ferry it was on. There was a small sign for cabins numbered 7001-7400 and an arrow pointing down a narrow corridor. Ros looked at the cabin key: cabin number 7203. She set off down the corridor, which turned a corner and then another corner. At this rate, she would have almost walked to France, she mused. Eventually, she reached her cabin. She slid the card into the slot on the door and a green light flashed to show her it was unlocked. Finally, she was in. She dumped her bags on the bottom bunk and had a look round. It was quite a neat, little room – very compact – but there was a shower and toilet, and the bunk looked reasonably comfortable.

She decided to go and get something to eat and drink and then do a bit of exploring. Ros made her way to the self-service restaurant on the next deck up and chose a plate of smoked salmon salad, a bowl of chips and a small bottle of white wine to wash it all down. She wondered why she had never been on a ferry before seemed the most civilised and relaxed way to travel. After she had eaten, she made her way to the bar and decided to look at the directions that Janet, her boss, had given her. Tomorrow at 9 a.m., she was to meet Jean-Jacques Boden, her interpreter and guide. Rosalinde could speak a little French, but not enough, and in the small villages away from the main tourist areas hardly anybody spoke English.

She sat back and looked around her. There were a lot of lorry drivers – Spanish and French – and school parties with teachers already looking glum at the prospect of shepherding a load of teenagers for the next week. The teenagers, however, were having a great time rushing around, giggling and messing about. Some were playing on slot machines; some were trying to impress others on the dance floor. Rosalinde wondered where the teachers were that were supposed to be in charge, as the kids were starting to get a bit wild: probably in the duty-free shop, getting stocked up for the week of hell that was facing them! She thought how glad she was that she was not a teacher, mainly because keeping an eye on that lot with all their raging hormones looked like a nightmare to her.

She looked at the brief Janet had given her. There were two châteaux – both in Normandy, but one in Calvados and one in La Manche. The first one was owned by a couple in their thirties with three children. They had spent the last three years renovating it to its former glory. Their plan was to open it as a luxury hotel, so everything had been modernised very tastefully. Rosalinde liked the sound of this one and she was going to stay in the château as their guest. Then she turned to the other château. This one was completely different; it had been in the same family for years and years. It was owned by Madame Mathilde La Roche, who was in her late seventies. Nothing had been done to the château for years, apart from basic maintenance, and the château housed many pieces of original furniture and works of art. Rosalinde thought the two would make an interesting article and an excellent contrast in the magazine. She was really looking forward to getting started and decided, after looking at her watch, that it was time for bed, as she had a very busy few days ahead of her. On the way back to the cabin she stopped off at the duty-free shop to buy some perfume, chocolate, and a bottle of brandy.

At six thirty, she woke up to what sounded like a Viennese waltz, and it took her a few minutes to comprehend where she was and that the music was coming from a built-in radio in the cabin. Rosalinde hadn't slept very well; she found the vibration of the engine and the motion of the ship over the waves a bit unsettling and she could not believe she had been woken up at six thirty.

'Bonjour, Mesdames et Messieurs. We will be arriving in Saint-Malo in thirty minutes. Please vacate your cabins. Breakfast is being served in the self-service restaurant. Merci,' announced one of the stewards over the tannoy.

'Oh God!' said Rosalinde, and she sat up on the edge of the bunk. She felt dreadful, dehydrated and weary, but there was no time to wake up slowly – she only had half an hour. She quickly got dressed and cleaned her teeth and then practically ran to the restaurant to buy a cup of coffee and a couple of croissants. She took her tray to the front of the seating area, which looked out onto the harbour of Saint-Malo. It looked quite an imposing place with its stone fortress walls.

'Will all car passengers please go down to the car decks?' said the steward in English over the tannoy. Then she repeated it in French.

Rosalinde got up, gathered her bags and looked around to see that she had not left anything behind. She dug deep into her pocket for the boarding card that the stewardess had given her the previous evening: D6, it read. Looking up, she saw a map of the ship and located D6, the door that she needed to get back to her car. It was on the other side of the ship, so she made her way through the teenage school party and the lorry drivers until she found the staircase that led to D6. Ros descended the stairs with all the other car passengers, which took quite a time as some were getting on a bit and the stairs were very steep and narrow. Eventually, she made it to the door that she needed and popped through onto the car deck. Now she had to make her way through all the tightly packed cars, back to her car. Ros found her car and got in. It wasn't long before the row of cars that she was parked in started to move forward and off the ferry, and then straight into another queue for a passport check. It seemed to take ages and she was becoming impatient and also a little concerned, as she was due to meet Monsieur Boden in Pontorson at 9 a.m. and it was already 7:45. Rosalinde handed over her passport to the gendarme and he made a half-hearted effort to look at her picture. He then handed it back to her, waved her forward and, at last, she was free to get on with her journey.

She drove through the port and out into the town. As it was still fairly early in the morning, the roads were quiet and she could drive slowly. Ros was getting her bearings, getting used to driving on the wrong side of the road, and taking in all the very pretty scenery and flowers on the side of the roads and roundabouts. She had been driving for about fifteen minutes when she saw a sign for Le Mont-Saint-Michel. This was the road she needed, so she turned onto the main road driving eastwards. It was a lovely morning; the sun was breaking through the clouds and it looked like it was going to warm up later. As she drove along, she tuned the radio into a French pop music station and she wondered what Jean-Jacques would be like: would he be like David Ginola, the sexy ex-football player? Or would he be like most of the French men she had seen on the ferry – very short, dark and scruffy?

It wasn't long before she saw the road sign for the junction for Pontorson, so she slowed down and turned off the dual carriageway. She followed the road, winding its way through very flat, endless fields of lettuces and carrots, eventually driving into the town. Rosalinde was due to meet Jean-Jacques at a cafe on the main high street. As she drove into town and round the mini roundabout, she saw Le Bar Sportif on her right. It was a small café which sold newspapers and cigarettes – slightly run down and in need of a fresh coat of paint – but it looked fairly busy, so it must be ok, she thought. She decided to park in one of the many parking places along the main street and walk back to the café. As she walked along, there were one or two boulangeries, a pharmacy and a florist on her side of the street; and opposite a jeweller, beauty salon, and a dog grooming parlour, just in the small area that she had walked. 'Wow,' she thought, 'most things are covered in this small town.' She had already seen two huge billboards advertising a hypermarket.

'Bonjour, Madame.'

'Bonjour. A table please,' said Rosalinde. Her schoolgirl French escaped her for a moment and, after she had answered in English, she felt foolish.

'For one?' asked the waitress, who had started to speak English.

'Two please,' she replied. 'I am meeting someone.' Then she thought, perhaps he had already arrived. 'Excuse me, I am meeting a man here, who I have not met before. I believe he is a local. I wonder if you know Jean-Jacques Boden and if he has already arrived.'

The waitress shook her head. 'Non, Madame. I know Jean-Jacques – he is not here yet – but if you are meeting him, I am sure he will be here soon.'

Rosalinde sat at a table in the window where she could watch the door. She glanced at her watch: it was, ten to nine. She had made up excellent time on the drive here and was actually early, so there was no need to worry. She was sure he would arrive soon. She ordered a small black coffee and took out the brief for the first château, the one in Calvados. It looked like it was about fifty miles from Pontorson and they were to go there first, even though the other château was nearer. She wondered why, but decided it didn't really matter, as she had plenty of time and she really wanted to enjoy this assignment.

'Bonjour, Mademoiselle.'

She looked up and in front of her was a tall, good looking man.

'I am Jean-Jacques Boden. You must be Rosalinde Wilson. The waitress told me you were waiting for me.'

'Yes, I am Rosalinde. Sorry, you startled me – I was miles away.'

Rosalinde couldn't believe her luck. Jean-Jacques was gorgeous: tall, with slightly long, wavy, blonde hair, and quite athletic. He sat down opposite her and ordered a coffee.

'How was your journey?' he asked.

'Actually, I really enjoyed the ferry. It was very relaxing, and I slept well. The drive from Saint-Malo was beautiful and I found Pontorson very easily.' She was already starting to relax and enjoy this man's company. 'I see from the brief my editor has given me that we are to visit the chateau in Calvados first. How far is it and how long will it take to drive there?'

'It's not too far; it will take about an hour and thirty minutes to get there. I have arranged for us to go there tomorrow at nine in the morning. The owners, Mr and Mrs Jacobs, have kept a room in the hotel free for you and one for me for tomorrow night.'

'Oh, that's great! Where am I staying tonight? I would quite like to get settled and have a look round the town.'

'Of course. I have booked you in across the road at the Hotel La Manche. It is very good and clean.'

'Great. Well, I think I would like to go there now and freshen up.'

Rosalinde paid the bill and arranged to meet Jean-Jacques at 12.30 p.m. for lunch.

Chapter Four.

Guy had lain awake all night, trying to think of a way into the chateau and he had realised that the only way he could gain access was to pose as an official from either the electric or water company. He was becoming completely obsessed with the thought of some sort of treasure at the château. It was as if everything in his mind had fastened onto the idea that as soon as he got his hands on whatever was in the château everything in his world would be wonderful. He knew he must try to control himself, especially in front of Therese. He did not want her to become suspicious. It would not be easy to hide anything from her, as she was naturally curious about most things.

Guy had made up his mind to pose as an official from the water company, just so he could gain access to the chateau, then he would take it from there. First, he would need to work out a plan, and acquire a fake ID and some overalls that looked the part. This would take him a few days, but he decided not to rush things. Everything had to be done carefully and precisely.

As soon as Therese had left the apartment, he got up, showered, and made himself a pot of very strong coffee. Therese had left two huge croissants on a plate covered with a napkin; she did spoil him. He poured the coffee and carried it and the plate of croissants through to his desk in the corner of the sitting room. He sat down in front of his computer and switched. Whilst he waited for it to come to life, he dipped the croissant in the coffee and took a bite. It was lovely and buttery and he enjoyed every last morsel. When he had finished, he swept all the crumbs onto the floor with the side of his hand, with no thought as to who would clean them up. Guy took out his cigarettes and lit one – the first one of the morning – and it felt great. He sipped the strong, bitter coffee, stretched out and focused on the screen.

First, he clicked on the word processing programme, thinking he would make a template for a fake ID. Then he remembered he had no idea what an ID card should look like, or what the logos of either the water company or the electric companies were like, so he went onto the internet and typed in *identity cards*. Straight away dozens of different pages came up. He scrolled down, looking through them as he went. About halfway down on the second page, he found what he was looking for: fake ID! He clicked on it and up came the page *Make your own fake ID*.

He could not believe this was available on the internet. He started reading, gleaning as much information as he could. He reached into the drawer to grab a notebook and pen, so he could write down everything he would need. The first thing he would need was a photo, in which he would have to disguise himself. He would also need a copy of the logo of the company he was going to pretend to be from. Guy decided to go with the electric company because he figured if he posed as an electrician, he would need access to the whole château, whereas a water company employee would probably be restricted to outside. Next, he went onto the electric company's website and printed off a page with their logo on it. Now he would have to think up a workable disguise that did not look ridiculous, so he decided to go to the local men's wear shop in Avranches to see what was achievable.

Guy spent the rest of the day gathering together everything he needed to pull off the deception. He had disguised himself with a fairly discreet wig and some dark-rimmed glasses, not wanting to draw too much attention to himself. Then he went to the photo booth at the railway station to take some passport sized photos. As he waited for them to be developed, he lit a cigarette and leaned back against the photo booth. He began watching people, wondering where they were all going. Just for one minute, he wondered what the hell he was doing, and then all sense went out of his head, as he imagined himself richer than his wildest dreams and living the life of a playboy.

The photos popped out into the dispenser. Guy bent down to pick them up and smiled to himself; his own mother wouldn't recognise him. 'This is going to work,' he thought.

It was five thirty. He just had time to get home and assemble the ID card before Therese arrived home.

Guy hid his disguise in the back of his car; Therese would never look in there. He decided he would cook a meal and open some wine, then spend the evening relaxing with Therese. He hadn't really paid her much attention recently and he felt a bit guilty. Also, he didn't want her to become suspicious. He didn't really love her. She was ok, and she didn't get on his nerves. He had never loved anyone; he was too selfish and self-centered. Tomorrow he was going to the château, where he was going to pose as an electricity board official to gain entrance to the interior of the building and begin his search for the treasure that the Nazis could not find. How he was going to achieve all this he still hadn't quite worked out, but he felt sure it would all become clear as he went along. He just hoped the two bumbling old men would not get in his way.

Guy was ready: he had disguised himself, clipped on his false identity badge and loaded his van with a toolbox and a torch. His initial plan was to have a look around and suss out the layout of the château. As he drove to the château, he felt fairly confident in himself and was pleased with his overall disguise. He turned into the tree-lined drive and drove up to the front of the château. He had to admit it was a magnificent building. He pulled up, got out of the van and took his toolbox from the back of the vehicle. As he walked up to the front door, his boots crunched loudly on the gravel beneath him. He pulled the bell pull and waited. After a few minutes he heard footsteps echoing from inside. The door opened and a rather elderly, shabby butler stood in front of him.

'Bonjour, how can I help you?' asked the Butler.

'Bonjour, Monsieur. I am from the Normandy electricity company. I have been sent to check your electricity supply and the meter. Please may I come in?' Guy held up his fake ID so that Didier the butler could see it. He held it far enough away that it was only just visible.

Didier sighed – all this upheaval! All he really wanted to do was sit in his room with a cup of coffee and his newspaper. There would be no chance of that now. 'Oui, come in. You will have to follow me,' he said gruffly.

Guy followed him, through the huge front door across the hall and down a dark passage to the back of the house. Didier stopped in front of a plain, white door at the end of the passageway.

'The meter is in the cellar. You will have to go down the steps and it is on the right, about three meters from the bottom of the stairs,' said Didier, opening the door for him and switching on the light.

'Ok. I will be some time checking everything down there.'

'Fine. I will leave you to it. I have other things to do.'

And with that he strode off. Guy started down the stairs. He could not believe his luck; he had gained access to the cellar alone without the prying eyes of the butler, who obviously was not the least bit suspicious.

Guy found the electric meter and set out his toolbox, so it looked as if he was actually working, just in case the old man decided to venture down into the cellar to check up on him. He looked around: the cellar was vast, with stone arches and even what looked like rooms spreading out in front of him. He could not see all the way into the distance because, although there was some lighting, it was very dim and a lot of the bulbs were covered in dust and cobwebs. All around him there were boxes and crates and racks upon racks of wine bottles. The further away from the stairs, the worse the dust and cobwebs became. He decided that the old lady obviously hadn't been down here for years and the old man knew that she would not come down here, so he didn't bother either. There had to be something here. This place was unbelievable; he could hardly turn around for boxes.

He was becoming conscious of the time, so he checked his watch. It said 3:20 p.m. 'Right,' he decided. Twenty minutes would be his maximum time; otherwise the old man would start to become suspicious. His plan was to pretend to discover a problem with the electricity supply, which meant he would have to return to do further investigation in the cellar. It would also require him to check all over the entire chateau and outbuildings. Guy set the alarm on his watch for twenty minutes and decided to have a quick scan around the layout of the cellar, so he could get a good idea of the arrangement in his head. As he walked around, he coughed; the air was thick with dust and mould and, in many places, the walls were slick with water running down them. He didn't fancy spending a lot of time down here, but his longing for the wealth he thought might be hidden kept him going.

The further he went into the far reaches of the underground rooms, the darker it became. There were not many light bulbs dangling down from the ceiling and those that were working were very dim. A small amount of light came in from some small windows set into the top of the wall. These, however, had a grill over them from the outside; were covered in years of caked on dust and grime; and had ivy curling inwards, growing down the inside of the walls. Therefore, most of the light was blocked out.

The cellar was vast and some parts of it were much older than others, as there had been previous buildings on the site stretching back to the fourteenth century.

Guy felt cold. The cellar was damp and the further he moved away from the stairs, the colder and damper it became. It was like looking for a needle in a haystack – for a start he didn't even know what he was looking for! He tried to get some sort of bearings, so that next time he descended into the cellar he would not waste so much time. He glanced at his watch: ten minutes had passed already. At this rate, it was going to take months to search this cellar, let alone the rest of the house and outbuildings, especially when he had no idea of what he sought in the first place. The treasure, if indeed it did exist, could be hidden in a crate, buried in the floor, or bricked up in one of these rotten damp crumbling walls for all he knew.

A thought suddenly struck him that if he got hold of a metal detector, that could save him considerable time and energy. He would have to dismantle it, so it would fit into his tool bag, but he thought it was sure to save him some time and could well lead him to the treasure much more quickly. Again, he looked at his watch: his time was up. He switched off the alarm before it went off. Ok, he would have to come up with some story now, for the butler. Guy made his way back to the base of the staircase and gathered his tools back into the bag. He reluctantly climbed the stairs and opened the door into the corridor. There was no sign of the butler. He decided to walk along the passage to the kitchens and, as he walked along, he paused and leaned against a door on the right-hand side of the corridor. There was no sound coming from inside, so he opened the door quietly and slowly and stuck his head into the room. The room was packed with antique furniture, much of which had seen better days.

'What are you doing there?' the old lady's voice rang out.

'Pardon, Madame. I was looking for your servant. I am from the electric company.'

'Well, you won't find him in here. Didier? Didier!' she called out.

Farther down the corridor another door opened, and Didier shuffled out. 'Oui, Madame?' he said.

'This gentleman is looking for you and, when you have seen him, will you bring me some coffee please?'

'Oui, Madame, straight away.'

Didier and Guy left the room and closed the door behind them. Then Didier turned to Guy and said, 'You should not have disturbed Madame La Roche. I deal with all household matters.'

'I am sorry, but I was looking for you and I couldn't find you, so I began trying all the doors and that is how I came across her.'

'Very well. It was unfortunate – we will say no more about it. Now, I will show you out. I presume your work here is done.'

'No, I'm afraid not. There is a problem with your meter and I will have to return in a few days to carry out some repairs.'

'Oh, can't you do it now!'

'No. I do not have the tools or parts that are required. I will be back in a couple of days to start work.'

'Ok, I will see you out.'

Guy thought he should try to strike up a friendship of some sort with the butler, but he was at a loss how to start. The old man seemed to be quite a prickly character, let alone Madame – she was a rude old bat.

'How long have you worked for Madame La Roche, Monsieur?'

'Why on earth would you want to know that?'

'Oh, I am just interested. This is an amazing château – it must be a wonderful place to work.'

Didier sighed and shrugged his shoulders. 'Well, it was many years ago, when I first came here in the late 1950s – when Madame was a young bride with her new husband and then their family came along. It was a very happy home.'

'So, you have been here since the fifties?'

'Yes. Of course, there were many more servants in those days. The château was a grand place – lots of parties, all the rooms filled with laughter and fun. The La Roche family have lived here for centuries, but times change and so do people as they get older. Anyway, I must get on.'

'Yes, yes of course. I will be back in a day or two.'

As he got in his van and drove away, he was tingling with excitement. There must be something hidden in the château and he was going to find it come what may. The butler was a doddery old fool and a puff of wind would blow the old lady over in a minute. In two days' time, he would be back to begin his search properly and, if they got in his way, God help the

Chapter Five.

'Bonjour, Rosalinde. How did you sleep?'

'Fine,' said Rosalinde.

Actually, she had slept really well and had a wonderful dream where she had been swimming in a lake with Jean-Jacques. It was a beautiful day, very hot and sunny, and they were completely alone. He dived into the lake and grabbed her around the waist, drew her to him and kissed her passionately on the lips. Unfortunately, she had woken up at that point; however, she felt very happy and was looking forward to seeing Jean-Jacques again. They had gotten on very well at lunch the previous day and Rosalinde felt very attracted to him. She was hoping the feeling was mutual but decided, as it was a working relationship, to be cautious. She thought she would try to find out a bit more about him, because she knew nothing about him at all. Ros sensed that he was not married but could not be sure if he was attached.

They were in Jean-Jacques' car heading towards the Jacobs' chateau. The countryside was very flat and all the roads were ramrod straight. They passed through tiny, quiet villages with very run-down houses on the edge, making them seem like ghost towns. Empty streets and shuttered windows all added to the gloomy feeling, despite the fact that the sun was shining. On they drove, passing by endless fields full of cows. As they reached Calvados, the stone houses changed to a softer, more honey coloured stone, rather than the grey granite of the Manche region.

Rosalinde asked, 'Jean-Jacques, do you have a big family?'

'Oui, I have a mother and father and two sisters. They are both married, each with three children.'

'What about you? Do you have any children?' she asked.

'No. I have not – how do you say? – settled down yet.'

'Me neither,' she replied.

'Good,' she thought secretly. Rosalinde was finding Jean-Jacques more and more attractive. She knew she should keep the relationship purely professional, but if there was any hint that he liked her, she knew she would not be able to resist. It was not like her to be so impulsive, but there was something about him that was so irresistible.

Eventually, they drove into the village, which was very picturesque. The trees were all budding up and the wild garlic was flowering in the hedgerow. Jean-Jacques drove through the village and turned left up a country lane. He came to some huge, iron gates between two stone pillars. As he turned in through the gates and started up the long, tree lined drive, Rosalinde could just see the château at the end of the drive. It looked very grand in the sunshine; the newly refurbished roof shone like a new pin and everything, from the slates on the roof to the gravel on the drive, looked impeccable.

There were dozens of windows on the front of the building, all immaculately painted, and two huge, antique, stone troughs along the front wall filled with red geraniums. Either side of the front door were two spiral topiary trees in pots, giving the place a very grand air. Money had been spent here – no expense spared. Rosalinde expected the interior to be even more stunning than the exterior.

Jean-Jacques pulled up and parked near the front of the main entrance. Immediately, the door flew open and out ran a woman, whom Rosalinde presumed was Caroline Jacobs, followed by a small child and two barking dogs.

'Quiet, you two. That is enough! Hello, you must be Rosalinde and Jean-Jacques. Welcome to our chateau.' Caroline held out her hand for them to shake. 'I'm Caroline, this is Eddie, my son, and these two monkeys are Poppy and Clive. They are border terriers and, I must say, spoiled rotten by everyone. Do come in. That's it – bring your bags with you. Mark, my husband, is working in the vegetable garden at the moment, so if you don't mind bringing them in with you, it would help enormously.'

'Of course. No problem,' Rosalinde replied.

'Blimey!' thought Rosalinde. This woman was quite bossy, but maybe she was just well organised and didn't like wasting time.

'Just tell us where to go and we will get ourselves sorted. Then perhaps we can have a chat and discuss the photos.'

'Great. Well, come on in and I will show you to your rooms, and then make some coffee.'

As they walked into the main entrance hall, Rosalinde could see that no expense had been spared, from the beautiful, black and white tiled floor to the enormous crystal chandelier hanging in the centre of the stairwell. She could tell this place was going to be glorious and she had a slight panic, hoping her photos would actually do it justice.

'Room four for you, Rosalinde, and eight for you, Jean-Jacques. If you go to the top of the stairs and turn left, your room is halfway down the corridor and yours, Jean-Jacques, is just a little further on. If you would like to settle in, and then I will meet you in the salle de jour in about half an hour. That's the room over there on the right with the double doors.'

They picked up their bags and started to make their way up the stairs. The dogs came running straight at Rosalinde and nearly knocked her off her feet.

'Come here, now!' Caroline shouted. 'I'm so sorry, Rosalinde. They have absolutely no manners.'

'Don't worry,' said Rosalinde. 'They were only playing.'

The spiral staircase wrapped itself around the circular walls of the hallway and Rosalinde could imagine all the people from the past gliding down the stairs in wonderful period clothing. There were several old paintings on the wall and she stopped to look at one of them: it was of a family, probably from two hundred years ago. The proud mother and father were sat on a chaise longue and were surrounded by four children of varying ages. One of the children, a little girl of about four, seemed to stare out of the picture directly at Rosalinde. She was dressed in pale blue and had blonde hair set in ringlets. Her skin was so pale – she looked extremely delicate – and Rosalinde wondered what sort of life the girl had lived. The family was obviously wealthy, but in those days, there was so much disease and illness and very little medicine that even the wealthy lost children. They moved on up the staircase and the portrait was forgotten for the time being. As they reached the top of the stairs, they paused to look through an arched window, which took in the long view down the drive. 'That would make a great shot,' she thought and, although she was slightly weary from the journey, she could not wait to get unpacked and start taking pictures.

    She walked along the corridor to her room. Jean-Jacques passed her to reach his room and as he went, he said he would knock on her door in thirty minutes, so they could go down together. Her room was painted a very pale blue and all the furniture had been painted with an antique effect but was overall white, giving the room a very light, airy feel. On the bed was a beautiful quilt, very fresh looking, mostly a mixture of white, blue and green. A beautiful ornate mirror hung on the wall opposite the bed and Caroline had placed a huge bouquet of lilies on a side table, which meant the room smelt wonderful. She threw her bags down on the bed and walked over to the window to look outside. The window overlooked a lovely courtyard garden, where the sun was shining on several small tables and chairs that had been set out for guests. She opened the window and could smell freshly cut grass blowing in on the breeze. Rosalinde moved back over to the bed and started to remove her camera equipment from the bag. She loved using a digital camera, because she could see the pictures straight away and delete any really bad ones. As she sat on the bed, there was a knock on the

    'Come in."

  "It's only me. I was wondering if you were ready to go down to the salon,' said Jean-Jacques.

    'Almost. I'm just sorting out my equipment – I won't be long.'

    'Ok.' Jean-Jacques came into the room and walked over to the window. 'This is a very beautiful house, is it not?'

    'Yes, it is. I think it's going to be fantastic to photograph. I can't wait to begin.'

    'Let's go down now and start work,' he said.

    Rosalinde slung her camera over her shoulder and followed him out of the room. Everywhere she looked there was either a stunning view, an interesting painting, or an exquisite piece of antique furniture. They made their way downstairs to the grand hall, where they met Caroline at the entrance to the salle de jour.

'Coffee anyone?' she asked.

'Oui, merci.'

'Yes, please.'

They both spoke at the same time. All three of them laughed and Rosalinde thought it was a good start to their working relationship. Caroline poured the coffee and they all sat around a low coffee table, which had two plates of tiny pain au chocolat and pain au raisin.

'Please help yourself to pastries,' said Caroline.

'Thank you.'

Rosalinde suddenly felt very hungry and realised it was nearly lunchtime, but then thought if she ate a couple of these pastries, maybe it would keep her going, so she could get a few shots taken and have a late lunch.

'Well, where shall we start?' asked Caroline.

'I would like to look around and get a feel for the château – maybe take a few pictures to assess the light – and then I can choose the best areas and set up some more formal shots.'

'Ok. Some of the bedrooms are empty. If I let you know which ones and give you the keys, I can leave you to look around on your own, as I have dinner to prepare. Then later, we can have a chat.'

'Great. Would you like to come round with me, Jean-Jacques, and give me your input?'

'Yes, of course. I would love to.'

Rosalinde finished her coffee and got up. 'Right, let's get to work.'

They spent the afternoon going all over the château. They went from the cellars to the roof, quite literally. Rosalinde managed to take several preparatory shots and work out more or less what she would like to photograph. There certainly was no shortage of amazing vistas. At 6 p.m., they decided to call it a day and retire to their rooms to shower and change.

'I will see you down in the courtyard at seven o'clock for an aperitif,' said Rosalinde.

'Oui, Rosalinde, see you soon,' replied Jean-Jacques.

In her room, Rosalinde kicked off her shoes and laid back on the bed. She was really enjoying herself. The place was amazing, and she felt a real connection with Jean-Jacques. 'I hope he is feeling the same,' she mused. He was quite difficult to read, but then she reminded herself she had only known him for a very short time. Rosalinde looked at her watch and it was already half past six. She jumped up and dashed into the bathroom to have a shower.

When she arrived down in the courtyard, Jean-Jacques was already there waiting for her. He had ordered them both a Kir and there was a small plate of olives on the table.

'What is a Kir? I've never had one before,' asked Rosalinde.

'Well, it can be white wine and Cassis, which is blackcurrant liqueur, or it can be made with cider and liqueur – that is called a Kir Normande. But this is really a Kir Royale, because it is made with Champagne,' said Jean-Jacques.

Rosalinde took a sip. 'Wow, it's lovely!'

She felt so relaxed; it was more like being on holiday than work. The evening was warm and they sat outside to eat, Caroline and her husband, Mark, serving them a fantastic dinner, which included homegrown vegetables and fruit. After dinner, they took their coffee indoors to the salon and discussed the plan for the next day. Rosalinde wanted to get started straight after breakfast, so they agreed to get up for breakfast at 8 a.m.

After a generous breakfast of fresh croissants and strong coffee, they set up and started photographing the outside of the château. It was a lovely, sunny morning and the château looked stunning. The photos were coming on really well. Rosalinde had taken hundreds of shots of the garden and the outside of the building. Jean-Jacques had carried her bags, helped to set up tripods, and fetched and carried for her all morning. By lunchtime they had finished preliminary shots of the outside, so they broke to have something to eat. Again, they sat outside in the courtyard.

Rosalinde was starving by the time she sat down with Jean-Jacques and Caroline. She was thrilled to see the table laden with French bread, cheese, salads, local ham, and a bottle of chilled cider – a local speciality, according to Caroline.

'So, how's it going?' asked Caroline.

'It's going extremely well,' Rosalinde replied. 'This afternoon we can start shooting the inside. Obviously, I'm not going to photograph the whole château, so I've chosen two of the bedrooms on the second floor, the salon, salle de jour and two of the bathrooms, which will be more than enough for my editor to choose from.'

'Great. I'm so excited! I can't wait to see it in the magazine," said Caroline. 'Hopefully, it should be great for business.'

'Yes, I'm sure it will," said Jean-Jacques. 'I must say, I'm very much enjoying this job. This is a wonderful place and the company is lovely.'

As he said this, he was gazing straight at Rosalinde, who realised he was talking about her and she started to blush. Caroline had not missed the exchange either, but decided to keep quiet. She thought they would make a lovely couple and felt quite excited for them. They finished with coffee and then went off to continue their work.

The afternoon sped by and soon all the photos were done. Rosalinde packed all the equipment away and then decided to have a bath in the wonderful rolled top bath in her ensuite bathroom. She was tired but happy. As she poured some very exotic, perfumed bath oil into the running water, she reflected on the day's work: she felt she had done a good job of capturing the château at its best and she had really enjoyed working with Jean-Jacques. She hoped she wasn't imagining it, but she was sure she could feel some vibes coming from him, especially after the look he had given her at lunchtime. Rosalinde enjoyed luxuriating in the bath. She decided Caroline and Mark had done a fabulous job of renovating this château; it was relaxing and luxurious. They had thought of everything. She got out of the bath and dried herself on one of the biggest, fluffiest towels she had ever seen. As she dressed, she wished she had brought better clothes with her but as this was a work trip, she hadn't thought it necessary. She had no idea she was going to meet someone like Jean-Jacques.

It was time to go down to dinner. They were eating in the dining room tonight, as Caroline wanted to show off her silver service skills, and Rosalinde was really looking forward to it. There was a knock on the door. She opened it and Jean-Jacques was standing there. He had showered and changed; he looked and smelt wonderful and Rosalinde was slightly overcome for a moment, but she managed to compose herself.

'Are you ready to go down? I thought I would walk you down, if that's ok," said Jean-Jacques.

'Yes, I'm ready. That would be lovely.'

Caroline was waiting for them at the entrance to the dining room with two glasses of Champagne. 'Here you are. Do come in. This is your table by the window.' She led them across to a table set for two.

'Oh, I thought you and Mark were dining with us tonight,' said Rosalinde.

'I'm sorry, but something has come up and we are unable to dine with you. I hope you don't mind,' she said.

Rosalinde gave her a sideways glance and she had a feeling Caroline had invented an excuse, so that the two of them would be left alone.

'No, not at all,' they both said together.

All three of them laughed and then Caroline walked away to fetch some menus.

The two of them had a fabulous meal and finished off the bottle of Champagne that Caroline had opened. After coffee and some very nice homemade truffles, it was time to turn in for the night.

'We will need to leave at about ten thirty in the morning, Rosalinde, because we have a fairly long drive ahead of us.'

'That's fine – I'm all packed up. We can have a more leisurely breakfast than we had today and then hit the road,' said Rosalinde. 'Actually, I'm shattered! I think it's time to turn in for the night.'

'Ok, Rosalinde. Bonne nuit. À bientôt.'

Chapter Six.

Rosalinde packed the last bag into the car and turned to say goodbye to Caroline and Mark. 'Thank you for a great time. Even though I've been working, it's felt like a mini holiday. It's so relaxing here.'

'No, thank you! We can't wait to see our château in the magazine. It's been so exciting having you here,' said Caroline.

'I will ring you and let you know how the pictures have turned out and I will send you a preview copy of the magazine.'

Jean-Jacques came down the steps of the château and shook hands with Caroline and Mark. 'Thanks, I've had an amazing time. You've got a wonderful place here and I wish you much success.'

Then he and Rosalinde climbed into the car and waved goodbye.

'That was really good. They are a lovely couple and they have a beautiful home,' said Rosalinde.

'Oui, they were very hospitable,' replied Jean-Jacques.

He started the car and drove off down the gravel drive. They were both very quiet this morning, lost in their own thoughts.

They were due at Château La Roche after lunch. Jean-Jacques drove and Rosalinde relaxed, thinking back over the last couple of days. She loved this part of France: the big, wide, open spaces; lush, green grass; and for the most part deserted roads. Every now and then they passed through a small village where the streets were empty, as at this time of day most people would be at work or school, but there was usually someone walking the empty streets with a baguette tucked under their arm.

'Shall we stop for lunch in Avranches?' asked Jean-Jacques.

'Yes, that sounds lovely. Do you know anywhere that's good?'

'Oui. There is a small café – near the big church – with one or two tables outside. Actually, it is a chocolaterie and boulangerie, but the lady who runs it does fantastic pizzas and salads and lovely homemade ice creams.'

'Mmm, I like the sound of that! Let's go there.'

'Ok.' Jean-Jacques glanced at his watch. 'We should be there in about twenty minutes.'

He drove into the square and parked in one of the bays in front of the church. The sun was just visible through the gaps between the buildings and the front of the café was bathed in sunlight. As they walked across the street, the café owner came out to clear one of the tables. She collected up the plates and glasses and looked across at them as they got closer.

'Bonjour, Madame. Un table pour deux, s'il vous plaît.'

'Oui. Please take a seat and I will get you some menus.'

When they were settled, Rosalinde looked over the menu and decided on a paysanne salad and a small carafe of white wine; Jean-Jacques decided to have a margarita pizza. He ordered for both of them and, when the waitress had gone back inside, he lent across the table to Rosalinde and caught hold of her hand. Rosalinde was slightly taken aback but thrilled at the same time.

'Rosalinde, I have really enjoyed spending these last few days with you.'

Rosalinde was completely taken off guard and felt very flustered. 'Um, oh – I – I feel very much the same,' she managed to stammer, and she flushed bright pink.

'Do you think we could get together when we have finished work? I would really like that.'

'Oh yes, I would like that too.'

Secretly, Rosalinde was almost bursting with excitement. If Jean-Jacques felt half what she was feeling, the future was looking great. Jean-Jacques got up and walked round to her side of the table; then he bent down and gently kissed her on the lips. She shivered with excitement and they both looked deeply into each other's eyes and smiled.

The waitress returned with their lunch. Rosalinde's salad was a huge bowl with lettuce, potatoes, bacon, and a wonderful mustard salad dressing. Jean-Jacques' pizza arrived next. It was thin and crispy and smelt delicious. The waitress also put a basket of bread and butter on the table, which Rosalinde used to mop up the salad dressing from the bowl of salad.

They had a wonderful lunch, spending a lot of time chatting and getting to know each other, and they decided to get ice cream cones to take with them, so Jean-Jacques asked for the bill and ordered two cones to take away. As they walked back to the car holding hands, they were both very quiet, lost in their own thoughts about the future.

They drove out of Avranches and the countryside opened out in front of them; it was so flat and green. As they sped along in the car, Rosalinde felt very content. She pulled the file from her bag and started reading about the next château they were visiting, Château La Roche.

She read: "The château has been in the same family for around three hundred and fifty years since it was built and, before that, there was a Norman fort on the site. The Gestapo used it as their headquarters during World War II, and then it was returned to the present owner's father-in-law after the war. Although the château is not in very good condition, it is very charming and will make a good addition to the magazine."

'Oh great,' she thought. 'This means I am going to have to work hard on my camera angles to make the place look fantastic, even if it is falling down and in ruins.'

'We are almost there, Rosalinde,' said Jean-Jacques.

'Ok. I presume we are staying nearby and not in the actual château, as it is a private home.'

'I have booked us into a hotel in the next town. The château is out in the countryside, two or three miles from the nearest village.'

Rosalinde looked up and was about to open her mouth to speak, when she saw the château just come into view through some birch trees.

'Oh my God! It is beautiful,' was all she could manage to say, as she took in the pink stone façade of the château. The grey tiles were shimmering in the sunlight, on the many small turrets and the gabled roof. As she took it all in, a strange feeling came over her. 'I know this place,' she murmured.

'Pardon?'

'Sorry.' She tried to compose herself. 'I have had a very weird feeling: I know I have never been here before, but this place looks and feels very familiar.'

They drove along a little lane through some trees, and then they came to some farm buildings that looked very run down and almost as if they had been abandoned for a hundred years. Brambles had covered everything with their prickly, arching stems.

'It's like going back in time,' said Rosalinde.

They passed some ancient farm machinery and several old wooden wagons, which looked as if they hadn't moved for a hundred years. They drove in through the gates and down the long drive lined with tall birch trees, their leaves making the sunlight dappled as they slowly made their way along, stopping when they reached the front of the château. Even though the château looked a little run down, Rosalinde thought it was very beautiful. The climbing roses around the entrance were all in bloom and the fragrance was intoxicating. However, she could not shake off a feeling of déjà vu.

As they climbed out of the car, the front door opened, and a man dressed as a butler stood there waiting to welcome them.

'Bonjour, Monsieur et Madame.'

'Bonjour, Monsieur. Je suis Rosalinde Wilson.'

'Entree. We are expecting you. May I welcome you to Château La Roche. I am Didier, Madame's butler,' said Didier.

He had a very strong French accent, which was quite difficult to understand.

'If you follow me, I will show you into Madame's sitting room.'

As Rosalinde walked into the elegant hall, she was overwhelmed by the beauty and proportions of the château. The ceiling soared above her and the huge staircase wove its way up and around the circular wall of the hallway to a gallery filled with large paintings. At the centre of the round hallway was an elegant round table with an oversized bowl of lilies on it, their exotic scent filling the room. They followed Didier down the passageway off the hallway and waited, as he knocked on one of the doors. He then announced who they were to Madame and showed them into Mathilde La Roche.

Madame La Roche rose to greet them. As she looked at Rosalinde, it was as if a lightning bolt had hit her. Rosalinde looked so familiar, it completely shook Mathilde. She could not take her eyes off Rosalinde; she looked so much like her son, Louis, but Louis had been dead for twenty-five years. Was it possible that Rosalinde was his child? It would be a massive coincidence if Rosalinde turned out to be her granddaughter. She struggled to compose herself, but took a deep breath and tried to focus on the moment.

Rosalinde could feel something strange happening between herself and Mathilde. She had this weird feeling about the house and, as she stood before this elderly woman, she felt like she had come home. She shook herself and reminded herself she was a professional woman, who had come to this house to do a job, so she stuck out her hand and shook hands with Mathilde La Roche.

At that moment the doorbell rang. Didier excused himself and left the room to answer the door. He was not happy; all this coming and going meant more work for him. He was beginning to wish he had not engaged the two old men to work on the house, as they had hardly done any work and seemed to be constantly snooping about. He opened the front door to find Guy standing there – this was another thing he could do without!

'Bonjour, Monsieur. I have returned to carry on working on your electric wiring,' said, Guy.

'Yes, of course. Come in. I'm afraid I'm rather busy today, so if you could carry on by yourself, it would help me enormously.'

'Yes, of course. I know where I need to go, but will have to come in and out for a bit to bring in my equipment.'

'That's fine – just come and go as you please.'

Guy could not believe his luck. Never in his wildest dreams did he think it would be this easy. He walked through the house to the door that led to the cellar. He could hear voices and wondered who else was in the château; he hadn't noticed the old men's van parked outside. Guy opened the door to the cellar and switched on the light. In the bag he had a small metal detector. Placing the bag down carefully in the corner where it was dark, just in case the butler decided to check up on him, he then returned to his van to get the rest of his tools. When he came back into the house, he thought he could make out two women's voices; obviously, Madame had visitors. As soon as he got back into the cellar, he shut the door and set to work assembling the metal detector. It was fairly easy to put together and, within a matter of minutes, he had got it working. Once again, he laid out his tools near the electric meter and then, armed with a torch, he set off to the far end of the cellar. The metal detector was working – he had tested it with some coins from his pocket – so he needed to make his way across the cellar systematically, to make sure he covered every nook and cranny. He was determined to find something and would leave no stone unturned. He was also aware of the time factor and, although the butler was obviously busy, he didn't want him to become suspicious. He set the alarm on his watch for thirty minutes and then set to work sweeping the metal detector back and forth across the stone floor. Guy knew that there was a very slight chance that he would find something, but his need was great, so even the slightest chance was better than none. As he worked, listening carefully for the smallest beep from the machine, he knew if he didn't find anything down here in the cellar, he would have to come up with some excuse to enter the other rooms in the château.

 Meanwhile, far above Guy, Rosalinde was unloading her equipment to start photographing the château. She had arranged with Mathilde that she should explore the whole of the château first and then make a decision about which areas to photograph. Rosalinde decided to begin at the top of the château and work her way down.

 It was an amazing place. The top floor looked as if no one had been near it for years. There were several rooms, which in the past had been the servants' quarters – quite small rooms under the eaves, each with a single iron bed and a very thin mattress. Rosalinde thought the rooms were pretty grim – bare floorboards and a bowl for washing in. The rooms would have been boiling in the summer and freezing in the winter. There was a toilet on the top floor, however, which was a lot better than many servants were used to. Even though it was a bit grim, Rosalinde thought it was very atmospheric and a good place to take a few pictures. As she worked her way around the château, the contrast between the servants' quarters and the family's rooms became more apparent. Although now faded in grandeur, the opulence of the main rooms of the château was still there to be seen. She would need to pick her camera angles very carefully to not show too much wear and decay.

 Rosalinde entered the main bedroom on the second floor. It had not been used for years – probably over one hundred years or more. It was beautiful. There was a large four poster bed and the walls were covered in faded, blue silk. She turned round to look at a large painting on the wall opposite the bed, and what she saw took her breath away. It was an eighteenth-century painting of the Comte and Comtesse La

Roche and their three children sitting around in their finest clothes, drinking hot chocolate from a silver pot. What shocked her was that the young Comtesse was the image of Rosalinde herself. She stood still in front of the painting, holding her breath, looking directly into the eyes of the Comtesse. 'This can't be true,' she told herself. 'You're imagining it.' There was no denying it, though; they could have been twins. She stood there for several minutes wondering what to do. She just could not let the feeling go. The painting was one thing, but then there was the feeling of déjà vu she had experienced from the minute she had arrived at the château. Rosalinde was going to have to say something to Mathilde, but had no idea how to bring it up.

There was a knock on the door and it opened. Jean-Jacques put his head around the door. 'Hi are you ok?' he asked.

As he walked into the room, his eyes were drawn to the painting. 'Wow, that's amazing – the woman in the painting could be you, Rosalinde!'

'I know. I'm not sure what's going on. I keep having a feeling of déjà vu, and now this painting – it's kind of creepy.'

'Rosalinde, do you know if you have any family in this part of France? You could be related to the La Roche family.'

'I have no idea, to be honest. I'm feeling completely bewildered. It must just be a coincidence.'

'I don't know. Maybe you should ask Madame La Roche.'

Rosalinde felt very confused. Should she ask this woman that she had only just met if they were related? Surely, she would think Rosalinde was mad. It was preposterous – there was absolutely no way it could be true!

Rosalinde decided to confront Madame La Roche as soon as possible, because she really felt her feelings could not be ignored. She also felt she would not be able to work properly with all this stuff whizzing about in her head. Maybe she should talk to her mother first; she might know what was going on.

'Jean-Jacques, I'm going to ring my mother tonight and ask her if she knows anything about this château and the family La Roche.'

'I think that is a good idea. Is there anything I can do to help?'

'Thank you. I think it might be a good idea if we go to the hotel now and then we can come back tomorrow, after I have spoken to my mum.'

'Ok, that's fine. I will go down and tell Madame that we are leaving now and that we will return tomorrow.'

'Ok, I will meet you down by the car.'

Rosalinde took one last look at the portrait before she left, trying to make some sense of everything, but she kept coming back to the same conclusion: that this was no coincidence. She just had a gut feeling that, somehow, she was connected to this château and the La Roche family. She closed the door on the bedroom and started to make her way downstairs, looking all around her as she walked along the corridors. The château was beautiful but very neglected. When it had been built, no expense had been spared, obviously, but that was a long time ago. Decay and sadness hung in the air. Once, these rooms had been filled with laughter and the sound of children playing. Their parents would have held sophisticated parties and entertained the nobility of France. She glanced through a window looking out across the garden, and she could see in her mind the elegant ladies in their fine, silk clothes and the men in their frock coats, promenading through what would have been the interwoven paths of a symmetrically laid out garden.

She shook herself and came back to the present. 'I must get downstairs and out of this house without seeing Mathilde,' she thought. 'I can't face her at the moment.' She ran down the stairs as quickly and quietly as she could. As she got to the ground floor, a man was coming along the corridor. 'Oh no!' She really didn't want to have to talk to anyone. She kept her head down and tried to get away without bumping into him, but he changed direction and started to come straight towards her.

'Bonjour, Madame,' said Guy.

'Bonjour,' she quietly replied.

Rosalinde then ran out to the car, where Jean-Jacques was waiting for her. She jumped in and they drove away, not realising they were being watched by Guy.

Guy was intrigued to know who this beautiful young woman was and hoped that she would not get in his way.

Mathilde La Roche was also watching as Rosalinde was driven away. She had growing concerns that something was about to change. There was no denying Rosalinde's likeness to her family; the resemblance was incredible.

Chapter Seven.

Guy was becoming despondent. His search of the cellar had resulted in nothing and yet he felt he could not give up. He had gone over and over the cellar floor and found nothing but a few rusty nails. The search had taken all day and he was filthy and exhausted. He sat on the bottom step in the cellar with his head in his hands, wondering what to do next. He wouldn't give up. He felt the treasure was here somewhere, but it was going to be a much harder job to find it than he had first thought. His trouble was that he was lazy, and he knew it: he always wanted the easy outcome with as little effort on his part as possible. This time he was going to have to be clever and careful. Otherwise Therese, his girlfriend, and Madame La Roche would become suspicious. He was also concerned about the young couple that had appeared at the château; he really didn't need other people getting in his way. At least the two old men that had led him here were not around anymore; he had heard the butler sack them earlier in the day and he had told them not to return. Guy didn't know what they had done to earn the wrath of the butler, but they were now long gone. He decided to call it a day and go home. He gathered up his tools and loaded them up into the van.

Guy had also seen the young couple leave earlier. The woman did not look very happy. He had no idea why – he didn't even know what they were doing here. Tomorrow he would return, and he would tell the butler he would need access to the rest of the château. He would make up a tale about checking the wiring. If only he could get a plan of the château; that would really help him find his way around. He could ask the butler, but he didn't want to draw attention to himself.

No, he would go home and sleep on it and come back tomorrow, feeling refreshed. Guy lit a cigarette and started the engine of the van. He hoped Therese wasn't home when he got in, as he needed a bit of time to unwind and he would have to come up with a story to tell her about today.

Rosalinde and Jean-Jacques arrived at the hotel and checked in. Ros wanted to go straight up to her room. Her mind was whirling, and she needed to speak to her mother as quickly as possible. She sat on the bed, not even noticing the room around her. 'I must calm down before I ring Mum,' she thought. She decided to unpack some of her belongings and have a shower before she rang her mother. It would help to calm her. The bathroom was small but very smart, with new fittings and a fabulously modern shower. After she showered, she opened a small bottle of white wine that had been left in the room for her. It wasn't chilled, but she didn't really notice. She sat on the bed in her dressing gown. Rosalinde drank half a glass of wine and then rang her mother's number from her mobile phone.

'Hello?' Ellen Wilson answered the phone.

'Hello, Mum, it's me. How are you?'

'Hi, Ros. I'm fine. How are you getting on in France?' said Ellen, guardedly.

'Well, it's really lovely here. Everyone is friendly and the scenery is beautiful.'

She was struggling to keep up a normal conversation, but she didn't want to just blurt straight out with masses of questions. It was no good; she was just going to have to tell her mother about the château and, in particular, the painting. 'Mum, I'm not sure how to say this, so I will just come out with it. In Château La Roche there is a painting of a woman from the eighteenth century and, well, it could be me – the likeness is startling. Do you know if our family has any connections to this area? Because I have had an awful feeling of déjà vu as well.'

Ellen took a deep breath. This was the moment she had been dreading for twenty-seven years. She knew that one day she would have to tell Rosalinde the truth about the past. Well, there was no escape now; she was going to have to tell her and she wished she was with her and not at the end of a telephone line. 'Darling, I should have told you everything years ago, but I was a coward. I suppose I thought you would judge me, and I also had other reasons, so I kept putting it off.'

'Mum, you are scaring me a bit!'

'I'm sorry. It's a very long story, which I really don't want to tell you over the phone.'

'Well, can you tell me something, at least? Like, is it possible that I am related to the people at Château La Roche?'

'Yes, I can and yes, you are.'

'How, for goodness' sake?'

'I know I have never told you about your father, and I am sorry I have kept it a secret for all these years. Your father was Louis La Roche, the son of Mathilde La Roche, who owns the chateau that you are photographing. I won't go into the whole story now, but he and I had an affair. A few weeks later, he was killed in a car crash and then I found out I was pregnant. He was married, so as you can imagine, I was in a bit of a state – I didn't know what to do. Eventually, I decided I would have my baby on my own and I would not reveal who the father was, mainly because I thought they might take you away from me.'

'Oh, Mum, I had no idea. I wish you had told me before.'

'I was going to tell you before you went to France, but you didn't ring me back. Anyway, I thought the chances of you actually going to Château La Roche were pretty small. How wrong could I have been?' she said, despairingly.

'Oh, God! That means Mathilde is my grandmother!'

'Yes, it does. Obviously, I never met her. In fact, she doesn't know about me or you, because I kept the secret.'

'What on earth am I going to do? I can't go back there, knowing what I now know.'

'I think it's probably time for the secret to come out. Maybe when she saw you, she could see Louis in you, because you look so much like him. What is she like?'

'She's fine – a little old lady with a wonderful chateau, which is starting to fall apart around her. You said my father was married. Do you think he had any children with his wife? I could have brothers and sisters.'

'Sadly, there were no other children and his wife was killed alongside him in the crash.';

'Oh my God! That means I'm her only grandchild. Wow! This is a lot to take in. I will be going back there tomorrow. Should I tell her who I am?'

Ellen thought for a moment and then said, 'Yes, I think she has a right to know. Please tell her I'm sorry I've kept it from her for all these years, but I was afraid.'

'Ok. I'm sorry, too, that you have had to carry that around all these years. How do you feel now your secret is out?'

'I don't know at the moment – a bit churned up. Talking about it brings it all back. Do remember one thing – I know having an affair with a married man is wrong, but Louis' marriage was a sham. He and I really did love each other, and we did plan on being together.'

'Oh, Mum, I don't blame you for keeping it a secret, but how on earth you have managed to keep quiet about this for so long is unbelievable! I'm sorry to have opened all this up, but obviously I had no idea when I took this job that this was going to happen.'

'Of course you didn't! I just feel really bad that it's happened like this and I can't be there to give you a hug.'

'Ok, Mum, I'm going to ring off now. I need to think this through. I will ring you tomorrow to talk some more.'

Rosalinde hung up and lay back on the bed. She couldn't think straight; her mind was all over the place. Then she remembered Jean-Jacques and that she was supposed to be meeting him downstairs in the bar before dinner. God knows how she was going to be able to act normally in front of him, let alone eat dinner. She made up her mind not to tell him what her mother had said. She felt she must tell Madame La Roche first; it was only fair. 'Right, come on. Pull yourself together and get downstairs,' she told herself. As well as finding out about her father – and grandmother, come to that – she realised she had fallen for Jean-Jacques in quite a big way.

She quickly dressed and put on mascara and lipstick and was just about to leave the room, when her phone rang. 'Hello?'

'Bonsoir Rosalinde. It's JJ here. I'm so sorry, but I have to go away urgently. My mother has been taken ill and I must go to her.'

'Of course, JJ – I understand. Um, don't worry about me – I can manage. Please let me know how she is, and I hope we can meet up soon.'

'Yes, of course. Sorry, I must go.'

Rosalinde sat back down on the bed. She felt as if she had been punched in the stomach. Of course, she felt for JJ – his mother was ill – but she was hoping he would help her through the next few days. Facing Mathilde was going to be hard enough with him by her side, but she was dreading it on her own.

She decided not to go down to dinner; her stomach was churning, and she didn't think she would be able to eat anyway. It wasn't long before she fell asleep, fully dressed on top of the bedclothes. It was a very restless sleep – she kept tossing and turning – and eventually she woke up just after five thirty. She felt dreadful! Her head hurt, her mouth was dry, and she had woken up feeling very apprehensive about the day ahead.

It was no good! She had to pull herself together and get her head straight. She was hungry – she would need to be fuelled up for the big day ahead of her – so she decided to have breakfast sent up to the room. She rang room service, ordered coffee and croissants, and then she got in the shower. Today was going to be a long one, so she needed to be on top of her game.

She ate her breakfast, thinking about how she was going to approach Mathilde. Once again, her stomach was churning. She decided it would be best to go straight to the château after breakfast and tell Mathilde as calmly and carefully as she could. Rosalinde did not want to give the little old lady a heart attack. After all, she was actually her grandmother.

Her car was parked in the car park. She didn't know how JJ had travelled to his mother's home, but she hoped he was alright. Before she set off, she sent him a text message saying that she was thinking about him and hoping that he and his mother were alright.

She drove towards the château. She felt so nervous she almost had to pull over to be sick. She knew that what she was going to say to Mathilde La Roche was going to change both of their lives forever. All she could hope for was that Mathilde would not throw her out without listening to the whole story. Considering her father was a married man when her mother conceived her, Mathilde could not be blamed for wanting nothing to do with her.

Rosalinde arrived at the château, feeling very apprehensive. She turned off the engine and sat for a minute, trying to compose herself. If she had looked up, she would have seen Mathilde watching her from behind the curtain of one of the first-floor windows. She was also feeling apprehensive; she could feel something was about to happen but was not entirely sure what. Ros got out of the car and walked up to the front door. Didier had heard the car coming up the drive, so he was already at the open door waiting for her.

'Bonjour, Monsieur,' she said.

'Bonjour, Madame,' he replied. 'Madame La Roche is waiting for you in the salon. She would like a word with you before you start taking pictures.'

'Yes, of course.'

Rosalinde wondered what Mathilde wanted to say to her, but was glad to be going straight in to see her. She climbed the stairs to the first floor and then walked along the corridor. As she reached the salon door, she took a deep breath and knocked.

'Come in,' said Mathilde.

'Bonjour, Madame,' said Rosalinde, as she entered the room. She could see Mathilde looked very strained and was concerned about how her news was going to affect her.

'Please sit down, my dear. I very much wish to discuss something with you that is very delicate,' said Mathilde.

'I, too, wish to discuss something with you, which is rather personal. Please would you let me go first? It may alter what you have to say to me.'

Mathilde drew herself up in her chair and said, 'Very well. Please go ahead.'

'I'm not sure where – to begin with – all of this, as it has only been revealed to me in the last twenty-four hours. However, I cannot continue to do my job without telling you.'

'You are going to tell me you are Louis' daughter.'

'What! How did you know? I have only just found out.'

'I knew the minute I saw you – you are so like him. I don't know how you are his child, but you are the absolute image of him.'

'Let me tell you what I know: yesterday, when I was in one of the rooms upstairs, I saw a painting of a girl that's probably two hundred years old and it could have been me in the painting. I was blown away by the likeness and I had had a very strange feeling ever since I arrived here that I was somehow connected to this place. I rang my mother last night and told her where I was, and she told me the rest of the story. I am sorry some of this will be painful for you and will stir up things from the past.'

'The past is past. Please tell me your story and don't worry about me. I want to know the truth.'

'Ok. My mother told me that she was very much in love with Louis and that he and his wife were getting divorced. She heard that Louis and his wife had been killed in a car crash and then, a few weeks later, she found out she was pregnant with me. She decided to keep the baby, but not tell anyone who the father was, and – this is a bit awkward – her reason for this was in case anyone tried to take the baby away from her.'

'Oh, mon Dieu! I would never have done that, but I can understand why she would think that, with him being the only heir. Rosalinde, this is a lot to take in for both of us and, I must say, it has shaken me to the core. However, I am very excited to know that I have a granddaughter and I am looking forward to getting to know you, if you feel the same way.'

'Yes, I feel similar to you. I am overwhelmed at what the last twenty-four hours have revealed. I can understand why my mother has kept quiet for all these years, as you do not come from an ordinary family.'

'My family is your family.'

'Please can you tell me about my father?'

'Yes, of course. Let me ring for some coffee, and then we can sit down and get to know each other.'

Chapter Eight.

Guy had seen the young woman arrive again this morning and go into "Madame's" room. He thought she was there to take pictures for a magazine but, so far, she had been holed up with the old woman all morning in the salon and no pictures had been taken.

He was becoming more and more despondent in his search. The cellar had revealed nothing, so he had convinced the lazy, old butler that he needed to check the wiring all over the house and he had started his search from the top down – right up in the top of the château under the eaves, where the old servants' quarters were. It looked like no one had been up there for years! The rooms were dark and filthy, stuffed with furniture and cobwebs. He doubted Mathilde La Roche had ever been up there. He searched the dusty room, looking for loose floorboards, any kind of alcove or hidey hole, where jewellery could have been hidden and lost in the intervening years. The job would have been easier if the place hadn't been so damn big – it was huge! As well as the former servants' rooms, there were several large storage rooms, all filled to the brim with furniture and boxes that looked centuries old. He was becoming obsessed with finding the jewels. He couldn't sleep at night or eat properly, and he knew that his girlfriend Therese was starting to become suspicious. He tried to keep calm, but he was starting to show signs of manic behaviour and all rational reasons were beginning to leave him. Guy had started to fantasise about confronting Madame La Roche, perhaps even threatening her to make her tell him where the jewels were. He had been at the château for several days now and he didn't think he could string his tale along for much longer. He was sure the butler was getting fed up with him and thought soon he would start asking questions.

Guy finished searching the attics and made his way down to the next floor. This was mainly made up of bedrooms and bathrooms again, which looked like they hadn't been used for years, but were on a much grander scale. The rooms were laid out like suites with bedrooms, bathrooms, and dressing rooms. Additionally, each had a small sitting room with shabby antique furniture, once very fine and of the best quality. He could not believe that the old woman had lived here all these years on her own, with all these rooms closed up. The rooms were all decorated at least two hundred years ago, with fine silk covering the walls and fancy chandeliers hanging from the ceiling. The chandeliers had been converted to electricity some time ago, so although the rooms were shuttered, he could see his way around. He worked methodically, sweeping through each room in turn. There were six suites on this floor and most of them were either wood panelled, or the walls were hung with silk. All the furniture was covered in thick drapes to protect it from dust and decay, so he had to be very careful to put everything back just as it was, in case the butler decided to check up on him. He looked at his watch and it was five p.m. He would call it a day for now and come back tomorrow. 'I must be getting close,' he thought. 'Not long now and I will be rich.'

As he was going down the stairs, he could hear strains of conversation coming from the salon. He tiptoed up to the door, which was slightly ajar, and put his ear to the door.

'So,' he heard the young woman say, 'should I call you grandmère now?'

What on earth did this mean? He thought Madame had no relatives. Who was this young woman? He thought she was just a magazine photographer.

'No, I think just Mathilde for now. We need to get to know each other a little first and I would like to meet your mother,' said Mathilde.

Guy wondered what was going on. This put a different light on matters. If there were going to be more family members turning up, he would have to either give up his search, or hurry up and find something. He carried on down the stairs and out to his van. The disappointment was starting to take its toll and he was no longer thinking normally. As he drove home, he became more enraged and decided he needed to come up with a new plan, but for now – this evening – he must act normally in front of Therese. She had invited her brother and sister-in-law round for a meal this evening and, although he was in no mood for entertaining, he would be a genial host and make sure the evening went off well to please Therese and stop her suspicions.

Guy stopped at the supermarket and bought some wine and some chocolates to take home for Therese. He felt an icy calm come over him, as he imagined how the evening would pan out. It was almost as if he were two people: on the outside he would be the friendly, jovial host, but inside his thoughts were becoming darker and more evil.

He walked into the tiny apartment. Therese was in the kitchen chopping onions.

'Hi, chérie,' he said, as he walked over to her and kissed her on the cheek.

'Hi, darling. How was your day?'

'Oh, you know, the usual. What time are Herve and Chantelle arriving?'

'At seven. Did you get some wine?'

'Yes, my darling, and I bought you some chocolates.'

He thought he was acting extremely well, because Therese seemed quite calm and happy. 'Yes,' he thought to himself, 'I can keep this up all evening. I will be Mr Charming himself tonight.'

'Right, I think I will go and have a shower and then I will come and help you lay the table.'

The evening went by fairly swiftly and, despite himself, Guy enjoyed it. Finally, it was time for their guests to leave and Guy was feeling exhausted; playing the congenial host all evening had tired him considerably. He and Therese waved them off from the window and turned back to look at the dinner table, which was covered with the remnants of the meal they had just eaten.

'I will help you clear up and then I'm off to bed,' said Guy.

'Ok, thanks. I won't be far behind you. I'm tired tonight. By the way, how are you getting on at the château?'

Guy let out a long breath; he'd been dreading this question. 'Oh, ok. There's still a lot to do.'

'Well, I hope the old lady is paying you well. You are spending a lot of time there.'

'Yes, yes of course."

In reality, he wasn't being paid at all, but if he found the jewels, he would be rich beyond his dreams. They finished clearing up and turned in for the night. Guy didn't think he could keep up his jovial act any longer, so he quickly got into bed and turned over and pretended to be asleep.

The next morning, he waited until Therese had left for work before he got out of bed. He really wasn't in the mood to talk to her this morning. Guy made himself some coffee and lit a cigarette. He sat down at the table, staring into space, wondering what on earth he was going to do. He could not keep up the pretense of working at the château for much longer. For one thing, Therese would soon realise there was no money coming in, and then there was the butler, who would also think the amount of time he was spending at the château rather odd. No, that was it. He decided that if he found nothing today, he would have to take drastic action. He needed to find these jewels and he was determined to find them at any cost.

Guy drove back out to the château and, as he drove along, he hoped the young woman was not there today. He thought he might be able to get into the old woman's room and strike up a conversation with her about the past. 'You never know,' he thought to himself. She might unwittingly reveal some information to him that could be useful. He arrived at the château, just as Rosalinde was getting out of her car near the front door.

'Bonjour, Monsieur,' she called out to him.

'Bonjour, Madame,' he replied, as charmingly as he could muster. 'Damn,' he thought, 'she's going to get in my way! I must focus on my task and not let her presence distract me.'

Rosalinde made her way into the house, thinking that whoever the man was, he didn't seem very friendly. She went straight to Mathilde's sitting room, where she was waiting for her. Mathilde rang the bell for coffee and they both sat down in big armchairs in front of the fireplace.

'Who is the man outside with the van?' she asked.

'Oh, a man from the electricity company checking the property,' said Mathilde, dismissively.

'Oh. He gave me a very strange look when I spoke to him just now.'

'Never mind him. Now, I would like you to tell me some more about yourself and your life so far. I want to get to know you and I'm sure you will have lots of questions for me too.'

'Yes, of course. Where shall I start?'

Guy carried his toolbox up to the second floor. This was one level above where Mathilde's sitting room was, so he would have to be careful not to make too much noise, in case they heard him and came to investigate what he was doing. This floor held a library and a ballroom, of all things. Who on earth had their own ballroom these days? He bet no one had been in the ballroom for years and he decided to start in there, as there was less to search through. He figured the library would take much longer, because there were infinitely many more hiding places. The ballroom was a large, rectangular room with six windows, three of which led out onto balconies, although they were all covered with shutters. Guy found the light switch and pressed it; the room was bathed in light from two magnificent chandeliers. 'Wow!' he thought. 'What a fantastic room.' It was painted a beautiful pale blue, with plaster detailing picked out in white and gold. Unfortunately, the room was being used for storage and it was full of furniture, covered in dust blankets. He made his way around the room, checking each wall for secret doors or hidey holes, pressing and knocking on the wall as he went. Once again, he could not find anything. His mood deepened and he started to have very dark thoughts. Why should this old woman have this beautiful château, filled with wonderful things, whilst he had nothing. He bet she had never done a day's work in all her life; she had just been lucky enough to inherit everything she owned. There must be another way to get rich or another way to find these jewels. Time was running out and he could not keep pretending for much longer. He decided to go down to the kitchen and get a glass of water. Maybe he could strike up a conversation with the butler and glean some information from him.

He made his way downstairs and entered the kitchen. 'Bonjour, Monsieur. Please may I get a glass of water?' he asked.

'Bonjour. Yes, of course. Actually, I am just about to make some coffee, if you would like a cup?' said Didier.

'Oh yes, that would be very welcome.'

'Ok. Sit yourself down and I will put the kettle on.'

Didier was quite pleased to have someone to talk to. Since Madame had discovered she had a granddaughter, they had been deep in conversation and he had felt a little bit left out. 'So, how are you getting on? Have you come across any problems with the wiring?'

'No. So far, so good. I have cleared the cellars, attics and the third-floor rooms, and I am currently inspecting the ballroom,' said Guy.

'Well, that's not too bad then. Will you have to look in all the outbuildings too?' asked Didier.

'Ah, yes, yes. I will at some point.'

'Ok, that's fine. Just let me know when, so I can unlock them for you. Of course, not all of the buildings have electricity – many of them, such as the old hay barns and the ice house, were built long before electricity was invented.'

Guy hadn't even thought about the outbuildings, and what was an ice house? It meant there was still a huge area to search. 'Excuse me, Monsieur, but what is an ice house?'

'It's a building underground for storing ice. It was used in the old days before refrigerators were made, so the house had blocks of ice for keeping food cold.'

Guy thought this sounded interesting and a possible hiding place, but he would have to come up with an excuse to spend any time in the ice house, as Didier had already informed him there was no electrical connection there.

'So, how do you like your coffee?'

'Black, please. No sugar. Have you worked here a long time Monsieur?'

'Yes, at least forty years.'

'You must know the place extremely well, if you have been here that long.'

'Well, yes, I suppose I do, but–' he hesitated, wondering whether to go on.

Guy looked across the table at Didier and could see he was wrestling with something internally. He waited, hoping that the old man would go on without having to be prompted.

Eventually, Didier spoke. 'I probably shouldn't be telling you this, but it seems Madame has a long-lost granddaughter, who has just appeared out of the blue.'

'Oh, that must be a bit of a shock for you all,' said Guy, feigning concern.

'It certainly is, but it is true – she is the daughter of Madame's long dead son.'

'And Madame had no idea she existed?'

'No. Apparently, Rosalinde's mother thought Madame might try to take her away from her, so she kept quiet.'

'Ah. Madame must be very pleased to have found her.'

'Yes, she is, as she has no other relatives. It is wonderful for her; I know she has worried for years what would happen to the château in the future.'

'So, Madame will leave everything to Rosalinde, you think?'

'Yes, I should imagine so. Well, it keeps it in the family.'

Now that Guy had the butler talking, he thought maybe he could ask him some questions without looking suspicious. 'How amazing to find out you are the granddaughter of a wealthy woman and that she owns a fantastic château that one day you will inherit.' He tried to keep the acid out of his tone; he didn't want the butler to know inside, he was seething at the thought of another one who was going to end up rich, having done nothing to deserve it, other than be born to the right people. " Will she inherit a title and money, as well as the château?'

"Um, there is no title. There hasn't been, since the Comte and Comtesse fled to England during the revolution, and as for money, you can see how we live – there is no money.'

'But surely, there must be something of wealth in the château – a painting or furniture, maybe even jewellery – that Madame may have forgotten about?'

Didier thought this was getting on dangerous ground. He had probably said too much; after all, part of a servant's job was to be discreet at all times. Madame would be horrified if she found out what he had discussed with this man. 'I really don't think so. Anyway, I must get back to work, and I'm sure you still have plenty to do.'

'Damn!' thought Guy. 'Just when I thought I was getting somewhere, he clams up.' He got up to go back to work, still seething inside.

Didier watched Guy get up and leave the room. There was something not right about him, but he could not put his finger on it. He decided it might be an idea to keep a closer eye on him. He knew there were rumours about the château and hidden treasure, but he had lived and worked in this place for decades – he knew practically every inch – and he had never come across anything that could be called treasure.

Chapter Nine.

Rosalinde had spent the morning telling Mathilde about herself and asking questions about her father. There had been tears from both of them – some sad, some happy – but now they both felt they knew a little bit more about each other. Rosalinde decided she liked Mathilde and she hoped the feeling was mutual.

Earlier that morning, she had telephoned her boss, Janet, and given her a brief explanation about what had happened. Janet had told her to take as much time as she needed and to let her know if, eventually, she would be able to carry on with the assignment, or if she would like to send someone else to finish off taking the photos. Rosalinde felt she would be with Mathilde for some time; there was still a lot more to find out about the family history and she wanted to fully explore the château. It was a fantastic place and she could not believe she was actually connected to it. She would finish the photos; there was no way she was letting anyone else do it. She was family now, so the place meant so much more.

Rosalinde had tried to contact JJ, to no avail. She was desperate to tell him what had happened, and she also wanted to know how his mother was and if he was ok. She really wished he was here, so she could talk to him about everything. Although it was wonderful finding out about her father and his family, it was also very overwhelming. She wanted someone with her, to hold her and help her keep from getting too carried away.

Mathilde had invited her to stay at the chateau, so at lunchtime, she drove back to the hotel to collect the rest of her things. She paid her bill at the hotel and put her suitcase in the boot of her car. Whilst she was in town, she decided to do some shopping and have lunch. As she walked around the town she felt quite at home and thought she would be very happy to move here. Of course, there would be lots of things to sort out at home – her job, for one – but as she travelled around to do it anyway, she couldn't see that being a problem. What her mother would say she did not know and, of course, there was Jake, her cat, to consider. She bet he would love nosing around all those outbuildings at the château, looking for mice. She was getting too carried away, imagining herself living at the château.

Rosalinde bought a bottle of Champagne to share with Mathilde, to celebrate finding each other, and some groceries to help contribute to staying at the château. She could see that Mathilde was not made of money and she did not want to become a burden to her during her stay. She knew Mathilde had a lady that came in to do laundry and cleaning, who – no doubt – would be fully employed this afternoon, getting one of the bedroom suites ready for her. She wondered who did the cooking; she felt sure it was not Mathilde herself, but couldn't imagine the butler doing it either. Rosalinde decided she would offer to cook for them, if necessary. After all, she would be staying there for nothing and it would be another way she could help out.

She drove back to the château after lunch. She could not believe how things had changed in the last couple of days. Rosalinde had left England looking for an adventure, but she had no idea anything like this was going to happen to her. Meeting JJ had been overwhelming and she kept reminding herself she had only just met him, but her feelings were running wild.

She pulled into a gateway, so she could try ringing him again. As the phone connected, she could feel her heartbeat getting faster. 'Please answer,' she thought. She hadn't spoken to him for a few days and she was beginning to wonder if he really felt the same about her as she felt about him.

'Hello?'

'Hello, JJ, it's Rosalinde. How are you? How is your mother?'

'Rosalinde, it's great to hear from you. I'm fine and my mother will be fine. I'm afraid she has had a stroke. I'm sorry I haven't been in touch, but it's been a bit difficult – I've been staying at the hospital.'

Rosalinde relaxed. Thank goodness he hadn't forgotten her! 'Oh, that's ok. I'm just glad you are ok and hopefully, your mum will improve, given the right care.'

'Yes, I hope so. Rosalinde, I have thought about you all the time – I can't get you out of my mind!'

Rosalinde was delighted to hear this and couldn't help smiling to herself. 'I feel the same, JJ. I can't wait to see you! Obviously, you can't leave your mum at the moment, but any idea when we might be able to get together?'

'Mum is going to rehabilitation next week, so I will be able to come back then. I can't wait to get back to you.'

Rosalinde was desperate to tell JJ about everything that had happened, but felt it was too much to go into over the phone. 'That's great. I'm staying at the chateau now, so when you return, just go straight there.'

'Oh, is the old lady ok with that?'

'Yes. It's a long story – I will tell you all about it when you get back. Look, JJ, I'm going to have to go now. I will see you soon, my darling.'

'Yes, my chérie. I look forward to it.'

She was so happy he couldn't wait to see her; that was all she wanted to hear.

She set off again and, as she turned into the driveway and saw the château ahead of her, once again she stopped the car. It really was beautiful and now, knowing she had a personal connection to it, she suddenly felt extremely overwhelmed. She sat in the car, crying great big sobs, as she thought of her mother and the father she had never known. What her mum must have gone through, trying to cope on her own with a baby and never asking Mathilde for any sort of help, because she was too afraid of losing her child. And then, of course, there was Mathilde, her grandmother, who had lost her only son in a car crash and had no idea she had a granddaughter. Mathilde, of all of them, had lost so much. Rosalinde had never had a father, so had never missed one, and her mother had, at least, had her child as comfort. Mathilde had been left completely alone in the world. But not anymore.

She dried her eyes, took a deep breath, and carried on up the driveway. She slowly drove up the drive, looking at everything with new eyes: the avenue of trees was coming into bud now that it was spring; underneath the trees, primroses and lily of the valley were blooming and the peonies were not far behind. She could hear the car tyres crunch the gravel below them in a most satisfying way; she loved how the old, stone garden walls were covered in lichen, all yellows, golds and greens, shining in the sunshine. As she reached the front door, she climbed out of the car and stood looking up at the front of the house. It was solidly built, but she could see it was looking a bit shabby; some of the windows were rotten and they all needed a fresh coat of paint. Mathilde obviously had done her best over the years, but it had become too much for her, both physically and financially. Rosalinde was determined to help her bring the château back to its former beauty. Between them, they would make this château great again. How on earth they would find the money to do it, she had no idea, but she was young, strong and not afraid of hard work.

Rosalinde took the shopping bags straight down to the kitchen and put all the food away. Didier wasn't there, so she couldn't ask him about dinner and if she could do the cooking. She decided to bring the rest of her stuff in and take it up to the room that Mathilde had prepared for her. Then she would go and see Mathilde and ask her about cooking dinner.

She collected her bags from the car and took them up to the room. As she opened the door and went in, it was like walking into a fairytale. The room was stunning; the decoration was pale green and cream. Mathilde had put fresh flowers on the table and clean towels in the bathroom. It was like a window into the past; all the furniture was antique, from the ornately carved bed with a silk canopy, to the side tables, dressing table and wardrobe. Thick, heavy curtains hung at the two windows and there were two oriental rugs on the wooden floor. Everything about the room looked perfect and as if it had been there for at least a hundred years. She thought it was about time she spoke to her mother again and so she called her number.

'Hello?' her mother answered, straight away.

'Hello, Mum. How are you?'

'I'm fine. More to the point, how are you? What's been happening? I've been dying for you to call.'

'Well, I really don't know where to start. Mathilde has been so kind, and I have moved into the chateau with her for the time being. Work has given me some time to process everything, although they still want me to get the job done. Um, the other thing is that before all this happened at the château, I met someone – a guy, obviously – who I think is really special and he feels the same about me.'

'Wow! Ok. I have got so many questions. What's he like, this guy, and what is his name?'

'He is French. His name is Jean-Jacques, or JJ for short, and he is my assistant for the job. But unfortunately, he has been called away, because his mother has had a stroke.'

'Oh dear! That's not good.'

'No, I know, but I've just spoken to him and it looks like she will be ok, with some help.'

'Good. Now tell me about the château and Mathilde.'

Rosalinde spent the next half an hour on the phone to her mother, describing the château and all its comings and goings. When she finally hung up, they had decided it would be a good idea to ask Mathilde if Ellen could join them, so they could all get to know each other.

Rosalinde looked at her watch: it was 5 p.m. 'I will go down and see Mathilde and ask her about cooking dinner,' she thought. Rosalinde made her way downstairs and into Mathilde's sitting room, where she was sitting by the fire. It may have been spring outside, but indoors it felt chilly and Mathilde didn't move around so much these days.

'Ah, there you are,' said Mathilde. 'I thought you had run off and left us.'

'No, of course not. I had to do a few things in town and when I got back, I telephoned my mother, to see how she was.'

'How is she? This must have brought back a lot of memories for her.'

'She is fine. In fact, she would like to meet you and is wondering about coming over to France.'

'Yes, I would like that. It would be lovely to talk about my Louis. She and I will have a lot of reminiscing to do.'

'Now, I would like to help around the house, and I wondered if you would like me to cook dinner for us this evening. I don't want to tread on anyone's toes, but I wasn't sure who did the cooking.'

'Well, Marie-Claire, who does the cleaning, usually prepares something for Didier to put in the oven. I'm afraid neither myself nor Didier are cooks. So, if you would like to cook a meal for us, it would be most welcome.'

'Good, that's settled then. Is there anything you don't like, or are not able to eat?'

'No, we both eat pretty much anything. As I have been on my own so long, it makes sense for Didier and me to share meals together – it's not much fun eating alone.'

'When I was in town, I did some grocery shopping, because I want to pay my way if I'm staying here.'

'That's very thoughtful of you, but unnecessary. We have a well-stocked larder and freezer – please feel free to help yourself to anything you may need. I will ask Didier to open up the dining room. It will be lovely to use it again after so long. We usually eat in the kitchen, or I have my meal on a tray here. I shall also ask him to get some wine from the cellar. Any idea what we are eating, so I can choose an appropriate wine to go with it?'

'Yes. I'm going to make a chicken casserole and mashed potatoes, if that's ok.'

'That sounds wonderful. Well, I expect you would like to get started, and I could do with a little rest. If you need anything, just ask Didier.'

Rosalinde got up and made her way to the kitchen. She liked the old lady; she was straightforward and didn't mess around. 'Much better to be like that,' Rosalinde thought. At least you knew where you stood.

The kitchen was amazing. It was a huge space, very traditional, with dozens of copper pans on shelves and an enormous butcher's block in the middle. It felt as if it was stuck in the past, but at least it had a modern stove, fridge and dishwasher. She found the walk-in larder and collected the things she needed to prepare the meal. Just as she was doing that, Didier came into the kitchen with a load of logs for the fire.

'Bonjour, Madame. I believe you are staying with us for a while.'

'Yes, I am. Thank you for making me welcome.'

'Not at all. You are family, after all. It is wonderful for Madame to have found you. She has been on her own for far too long.'

'Well, I intend to help around here. I'm not here to be spoiled and treated like a visitor, so I'll start by cooking dinner tonight. Mathilde asked if you would lay the table in the dining room and bring up some wine from the cellar to go with chicken.'

Didier's eyebrows shot up and his whole body stiffened.

'Oh, I'm so sorry, Didier – that did not come out how I meant it. I sound like a right bossy boots – like I'm trying to take over.'

'It's ok, Madame. It's just you are so like your grandmother – it knocked me back a bit, that's all. Of course, I will lay the table and fetch the wine. It will be a pleasure.'

He went over to the fireplace and took down a key that was hanging on an old, iron hook. Rosalinde watched him as he crossed the room to an old, wooden door. He unlocked the door and went through, switching on the light as he made his way down the stone steps that were behind it. She was curious, so she followed him down the spiral staircase into the cellar. He heard her following him and when he reached the bottom, he called to her, 'Would you like to have a look around? You're more than welcome. I'm just going to get some wine and then I must get on and lay the table. We haven't used the dining room for a while, and it will need a good clean.'

'I would love to. There is so much to explore, but I'd better not take too long – I'm supposed to be cooking! I will just have a quick look, whilst you are down here.'

Rosalinde was excited by the cellar. It was incredibly atmospheric and there was a lot of it to explore. She decided she would come back down in a few days with her camera to take some pictures and have a good rummage around. Now she must get back to the kitchen and make a start on the dinner. Whilst she cooked, she looked around the kitchen, making herself familiar with everything. As she chopped the vegetables for the casserole, she had to keep reminding herself that this was her father's home, where he had been born and raised, and although she had never known him, it helped her to connect to him. She decided that she would ask Mathilde if she had any photos of her father; it had occurred to her she had never seen his face. Her mother had never even mentioned him and always changed the subject when Rosalinde had asked.

Rosalinde finished preparing the meal and put the casserole in the oven. She decided to have a quick shower and then ask Didier to serve the chilled Champagne in the sitting room before dinner. On her way up to her room, she put her head around the dining room door, just to check everything was ready.

Didier had laid the table beautifully, with crystal glasses and a crisp, white cloth. He had even put flowers on the table. It was perfect. She only hoped her cooking would do it justice.

Mathilde was waiting for her in the sitting room when she came down after her shower. The Champagne had been opened and was cooling in a silver ice bucket. As soon as Rosalinde appeared, Didier came in and poured two glasses for them.

'If it is ok with you, Mathilde, I would really like Didier to join us in a toast.'

'Yes, of course. Please get yourself another glass, Didier.'

'Thank you, Madame.' Didier poured himself a glass and Rosalinde made the toast.

'First of all, I would like to thank you, Mathilde, for making me so welcome and accepting me as part of the family. This can't have been easy for you. As for myself, I have been totally overwhelmed to find I have a French grandmother and to find that you live in this most wonderful château. I hope that in the future we can build a strong relationship that also includes my mother. Anyway, enough of that. Please raise your glasses!' Mathilde stood up next to Rosalinde and Didier. 'To us!' said Rosalinde.

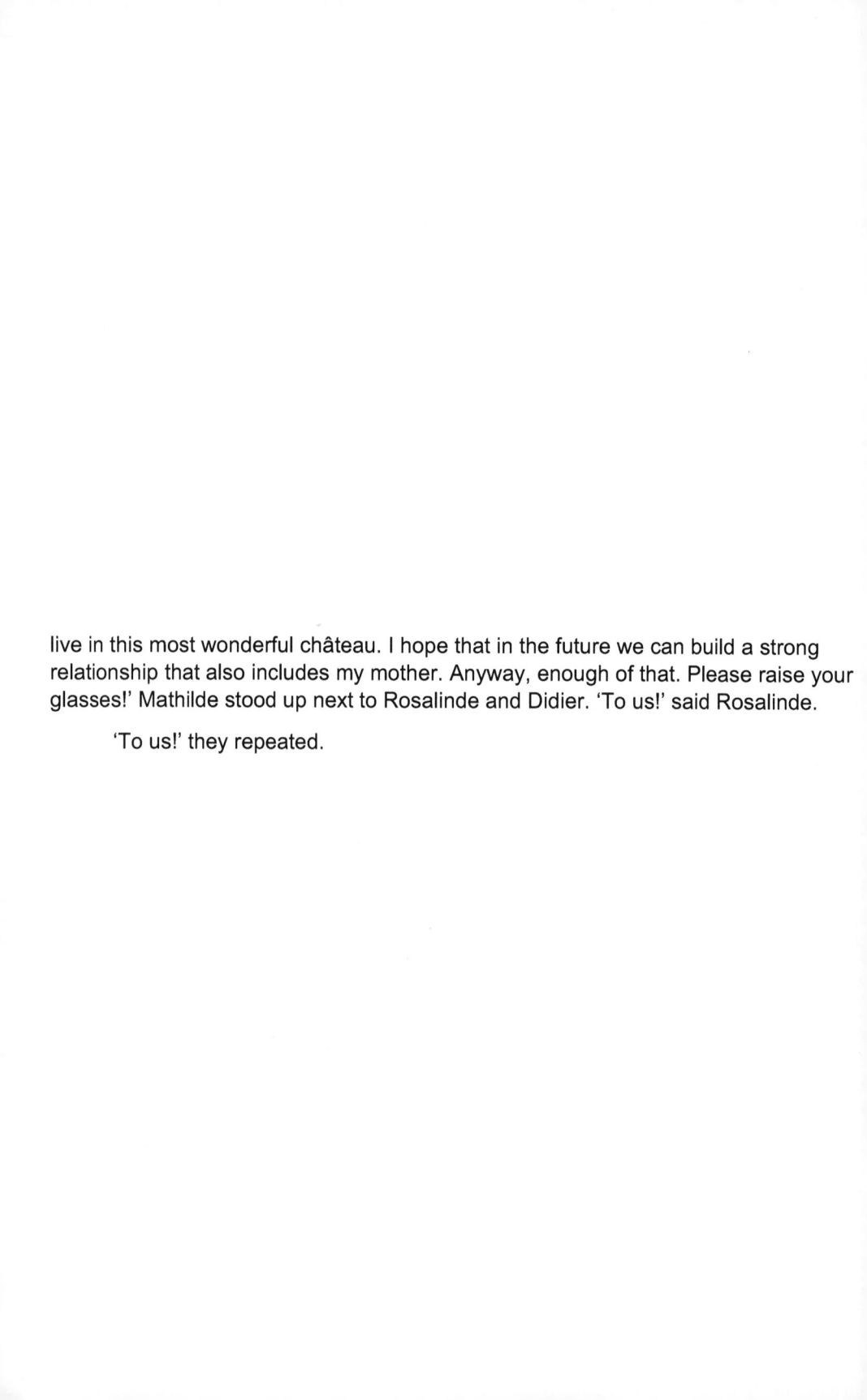

'To us!' they repeated.

Chapter Ten.

It was very early in the morning when Guy woke. He was losing it. He knew that he could not keep up with this ridiculous search; his life was starting to unravel. Therese was becoming suspicious and he was growing tired of leading a double life. During the night a thought had come to him: it was crazy, but if Madame was so pleased to have her newly found granddaughter by her side, maybe she would be prepared to pay a reward to find her upon her disappearance! He could kidnap her and hold her to ransom, and then the old girl would either pay up or own up to the whereabouts of the jewels.

It was madness, but it seemed like a good idea to him. He'd been into the cellars and the outbuildings; there were plenty of places to hide a person right under their noses. The beauty of this plan was that he could carry on pretending to check the electrics, whilst holding Rosalinde prisoner. Had he got the stomach for it though? He let out a sigh.

He arrived at the château at nine a.m. It was a beautiful morning: the sky was blue, the sun already high; and the air was so fresh and light. It was hardly the setting for a kidnap!

The birds were singing, but Guy hadn't even noticed. He went straight into the outbuildings furthest from the main house. He had already been in several of the buildings on the estate, but not this one. It was a stable with an upstairs loft. The ground floor was absolutely crammed with old junk. In the stable area downstairs, there was even an old carriage mildewed and dusty from years of neglect. He climbed the rickety stairs to the loft area. It was full of dusty bales of hay, which looked like they had been there for years. The stone walls were covered in huge thick cobwebs which made him shudder; he hated spiders. 'I bet there are rats in here, too,' he thought. Guy climbed over the bales piled up in the middle of the floor. As he did so, he disturbed a feral cat and her kittens. The cat hissed at him and arched her back. She didn't take her eyes off him, but she didn't move from her kittens. He skirted around the cat. He wanted to see what was at the back of the loft; maybe there was another room where he could hide the girl. The walls were so thick in these old buildings that he was sure, if she was tied up and gagged, no one would be able to hear her.

Guy was in luck! Right at the back in the far corner, there was a small, wooden door, about three feet high. He rushed over and attempted to open it, to see what lay behind. It didn't want to open – it was so stiff – but then it probably hadn't been opened in years. Eventually, he managed to drag it open, to reveal an under-the-eaves space about seven feet long by four feet wide. It was a perfect place to hide someone. He sat back on one of the hay bales and ran his hand across his face. 'Is this really happening?' he thought. 'If I'm going to do this, I need to plan it down to the last detail.' He pondered how he would get her into the stables in the first place. Then, how would he keep her there?

Just at that moment, he heard a voice out in the courtyard. He quietly moved into the shadow of the window, so he could look out and see who it was. It was Rosalinde, casually walking across the courtyard; she looked as if she didn't have a care in the world. Guy watched her as she crossed the yard and went into one of the other outbuildings. He noticed she had her camera with her and guessed she was photographing the outbuildings, as well as the château itself. Maybe that was how he could lure her to the stables: he could come up with a story about how fantastic the stables were and urge her to photograph them; then, once she was in there, he could trap her.

He would have to act carefully, and he needed to prepare. It was no good going out there now and telling her to come and look; he didn't have any rope or tape to tie her up. So instead, he got out his notepad and started a list: *sleeping bag, rope, duct tape, bucket, food and water, knife.* That would do to start with. He would go into town just before lunch and stop at the big supermarket. He should be able to get everything there. Oh, and there was one more thing: he thought of a padlock to go on the door.

He looked around the loft and decided to rearrange the bales of hay, to conceal the door. The bales were very heavy and so dusty that by the time he had finished, he was filthy dirty, sweating and coughing. He really wasn't used to hard work, but it would all be worth it in the end. Guy seemed to think that what he was doing was completely normal – he rationalised his kidnapper's shopping list as a means to an end – but really he was turning into a full-blown psychopath.

He dusted himself down and climbed down the stairs, looking at everything as he went; making sure he knew every nook and cranny in the stables; looking out for places he could hide equipment; and also checking out the view from the main house and other buildings. He would have to come and go without being seen, once he had Rosalinde held up in the loft. Guy walked out into the courtyard. The sun was so bright it hurt his eyes, after being in the dark, dusty loft. He looked around: there was no one, besides the feral mother cat, watching him with her hard, black eyes. It was almost as if she knew what he was plotting; she narrowed her eyes at him and hissed as he walked past. He shivered. He hated cats; they made his skin crawl.

Didier had so much to do, especially now Rosalinde had moved in. He wasn't sure that Madame had considered the impact of having another person in the house after all these years. Even though Rosalinde had offered to help with the cooking, there was still so much to do, and he was feeling his age. This morning he needed to go all around the house emptying bins, because the refuse men would be coming tomorrow and he liked to be ready a day in advance. The wheelie bins were kept around the back of the château in the old courtyard, so when he had loaded up two big, black bin liners with the rubbish, he carried them out the back door to the bins. He was just about to cross the courtyard when he caught sight of the electric man creeping around the back of the old stables. He stood and watched him for a moment. He looked odd – as if he was sussing the place out – but then Didier remembered he was there to survey the whole property, shrugged his shoulders and got on with the business of clearing the rubbish.

Guy parked his car in the loneliest corner of the car park. There weren't many cars parked outside the hypermarket, as it was almost lunchtime. He pulled a trolly from the long stack and entered the store. He had his list with him, but decided it would be a good idea to buy some other things as well, so it didn't look so suspicious. He went around the enormous, deserted shop fairly rapidly. He knew where most things were, so it didn't take long to complete his shop. Guy had added in some food and a bottle of wine for Therese, his girlfriend. He went through the checkout as quickly as possible, paying cash and not entering into small talk with the young girl on the till; he didn't want to be remembered. However, he needn't have worried, since she seemed extremely disinterested anyway. She hardly looked at him, as she passed the items over the scanner.

'Ninety-two euros, s'il vous plaît.' She held out her hand and looked up at him, expectantly.

He counted out the money and placed it into her hand, all the time not making eye contact. 'Merci,' he grunted and wheeled his trolly over to the exit.

Guy sat in his car, eating a baguette that he had bought in the hypermarket. He usually had something a bit better for lunch, but time was against him today. He finished the baguette and drank half a bottle of Coca-Cola. Now he needed to get back to the château and store the stuff he had bought in the loft, away from prying eyes.

As he drove back to the château, he was thinking about how he would entice Rosalinde up into the barn. As he had only ever said good morning to her, he realised he would have to try and start being a bit more friendly. She was a photographer, so maybe he could strike up a conversation about that and then tell her there was something to see in the barn that was worth photographing.

Luckily, the courtyard was deserted when he arrived back at the château. He parked as close to the barn as he possibly could. Sheepishly, he opened the back of the van and quickly took his shopping over to the barn door, pushing it open with his hip and dumping everything inside, before going back to the van for another load. When he had carried it all inside, he then set about getting it up the narrow staircase and stashing it in the cubby hole behind the bales of hay. He took a deep breath to steady himself. 'Right,' he thought, 'I'm ready. Now all I need is to gain her trust.'

Guy decided to go over to the house and see if he could accidentally bump into Rosalinde. He took his tool bag from the van and then went into the château by the back door. He was still allegedly working on the house and he hadn't even started to check the main rooms on the ground floor yet.

Rosalinde was in the main salon. She had resumed photographing the house for the magazine she worked for and had set up some shots around the fireplace. The light was filtering in through the half-shuttered windows, giving everything an ethereal look and feel. The château had a fragile, eerie quality to it, as if time had stood still for years. In a way it had. When Rosalinde's father had died, Mathilde had retreated into her home and had, for some reason, tried to keep everything the same. Rosalinde checked the frame; it was good, so she took the picture. Just as she pressed the button, the door flew open and a sheaf of papers flew off the table and ruined the shot.

'What on earth was that?' She turned round to see the electricity man standing there with his hand on the doorknob.

'Pardon, Madame,' said Guy. 'I did not know you were in here.'

'You have just ruined my shot!'

'I am so sorry. Here, let me help you.' Guy quickly bent down and started picking papers up from the floor, but he was a clumsy person and he managed to knock into a small round table with a vase of flowers on it, sending it crashing to the floor.

'Oh my God! Look what you've done now. Please get out, before you cause any more damage!'

'I'm so sorry,' he said.

Backing out of the doorway, he turned away and scowled. That was a disaster; he would never be able to get her to come with him to the barn now. He would have to think up an alternative plan, which would not be so friendly.

Rosalinde was fuming. She had spent ages setting up that last shot, only to have that idiot mess it all up in seconds. She was missing JJ; they had worked so well together at Caroline and Mark's château. He would have sorted everything out and kept her calm. She hoped he would be back soon. These last few days her world had turned upside down, in many ways for the better, but all this new information about her father and Mathilde and the château was a lot to take in. She reset the shot and took a few pictures, checking them fastidiously. The château was so beautiful and untouched that it photographed really well. Rosalinde decided not to rearrange too much in the rooms and keep the pictures fairly natural, giving them an eerie quality.

Ok, she felt she had done enough for today and decided to go for a walk in the grounds to explore, as it was a lovely afternoon. She was cooking dinner again this evening, but she had plenty of time to go for a walk and then come back and prepare the meal. Mathilde always had a rest during the afternoon, so Rosalinde slipped quietly out of the château without bothering to tell Mathilde or Didier where she was going.

As she closed the back door behind her, she had no idea she was being watched from the corner of the barn.

Guy was on the alert as soon as he heard the back door. He knew it wasn't the old man or the old woman; they were both taking an afternoon nap. Rosalinde had come out of the door, her long, blonde hair flying loose in the wind. She had walking boots on and had set off in the direction of the woods, alone.

It's now or never, he decided, and ran up to the loft. He quickly gathered the knife, rope, and tape and ran back outside into the courtyard. He could see her walking through the woods towards the lake, and resolved to follow her at a safe distance, but go the opposite way around the lake and hide in wait for her there. He kept well back, which was just as well, because every now and then Rosalinde would stop to take in the view or look at the wildflowers that were growing everywhere. She eventually came to the lake and turned left to follow the path round. Guy turned right and now he sped up, being careful not to make too much noise; he didn't want to scare her off. He turned the corner of the lake and there was a huge oak tree; it must have been six feet across. This would do as a hiding place. He leaned against the tree and took a large breath. Was he really doing this? There was no going back after this! Yes, yes, this was it. He got ready. He could hear her footsteps trampling the long grass, getting closer. He just had to time it right and then spring out from behind the tree. He held the knife in his hand, turning it round and round in anticipation. His heart was beating wildly. She was almost level with the tree. Now! He must do it now!

Guy stepped out in front of Rosalinde with the knife held high in front of him. She gasped, stepped back, tripped over and fell onto her back. Before she could get up, he was on top of her, one leg either side of her body. She was trapped. She tried to get up, but his weight was too much for her. She struggled and tried to knock the knife from his hand, but he was determined as he struck her on the side of the head, rendering her unconscious.

Before she could come to, he gagged her and bound her hands together. As she was quite light, he picked her up and carried her back to the barn, now and then glancing over his shoulder to make sure no one had seen him. Once he got to the barn, he dragged her up the stairs, tied her legs together, and shoved her into the eaves space he had prepared. He then put all the hay bales back into place and made it look as if it had never been moved in the first place.

He was exhausted and running with sweat, but strangely exhilarated, almost turned on, by what he had just done.

Chapter Eleven.

Mathilde woke from her afternoon rest. She sighed, feeling quite low in spirits, until she remembered Rosalinde. As she lay on her bed, the warm sunshine streaming through the window, she smiled and thought how lucky she was that Rosalinde had come into her life, almost selfishly just when she needed someone. Life was getting more difficult as she was getting older, and the constant worry of the château and her aches and pains had been getting her down for some time. She had already called her solicitor and arranged an appointment to make some changes to her will. She didn't expect Rosalinde to give up her life in England, but she had decided she would hand the château and all its contents over to Rosalinde immediately. Then Rosalinde could decide what to do with it. If she decided to sell it, that would be up to her; it would be out of Mathilde's hands.

She got up and went into her bathroom to wash her face and freshen up. She would then go down and see what Rosalinde was cooking for dinner this evening. She was enjoying having someone else doing the cooking and Rosalinde was a very good cook.

Mathilde entered the kitchen and was surprised that there was no noise or smell of a meal being prepared; there was no sign of either Rosalinde or Didier. She wondered where they could be, as it was six p.m. and no preparations for dinner had begun, as far as she could tell.

Mathilde went to her sitting room and rang the bell for Didier. Eventually, she could hear him shuffling along the passageway.

'Good evening, Madame. What can I do for you?' he asked.

'Didier, do you know where my granddaughter is?'

'Is she not in the kitchen, preparing dinner, Madame?'

'No Didier, she is not. I would not be asking you if she was, would I?' Mathilde said, grumpily.

'Oh, then I am not sure, Madame. I did see her go out for a walk with her camera earlier this afternoon, but that was several hours ago. I expect she has walked further than intended and will be back soon. She has probably lost track of the time.'

'Well, in that case, Didier, please would you start preparing dinner? When she comes back, I'm sure she will help you.'

'Very good, Madame.'

Didier turned and left the room. He was not too pleased that he would have to start dinner; he was enjoying the fact that Rosalinde had taken over in the kitchen. He hoped she would come back soon. He wasn't entirely sure what she had planned for this evening's meal and he didn't want to mess it up.

Didier shuffled off to the kitchen, feeling a bit cross that Mathilde had been grumpy with him. It wasn't his fault that Rosalinde had not appeared to cook the evening meal. He opened the fridge and saw that Rosalinde had already made some preparations: she had folded foil parcels with fish, white wine and herbs. 'Ok,' he thought. 'That's not too bad then. I can do some vegetables and make a fruit salad for dessert.' He got everything out and started work on the vegetables, quite expecting Rosalinde to appear at any moment.

Didier finished preparing the meal and went into the dining room to set the table. As he did so, he glanced at the clock: it was now ten past seven and Rosalinde had still not appeared. He stopped and thought for a moment. Had she said she would be out this evening and he had forgotten? It was not like her to be late; she was always very reliable and eager to help. He carried on laying the table and thought Rosalinde must have lost sense of time, but he did wonder if something had happened to her. He hoped she hadn't fallen and hurt herself. He wondered what to do regarding cooking the meal, as Madame was a stickler for everything running smoothly. It was all ready to cook and wouldn't take long, but if he started it and Rosalinde wasn't back, it would be ruined.

Just as he was pondering this, Mathilde came into the dining room. 'Is she back yet?' she asked. There was a small tremor in her voice, which Didier couldn't confidently define as either anger or concern.

'Not as far as I know, Madame. What shall I do about dinner?'

Mathilde looked at her watch: it was seven twenty. 'We will give her until seven forty-five, and if she is not back by then, you may start cooking.' Mathilde was becoming concerned. She was sure her granddaughter had said she would be cooking this evening. What on earth had happened to her? 'Perhaps you could go and have a look for her, Didier. Which direction did you see her going in earlier?'

'She looked like she was going through the woods to the lake, Madame.'

All of a sudden, it became too much for Mathilde. She put her hand to her mouth and let out a sob. 'Oh, Didier! What if something has happened to her? She might have fallen over and hurt herself.'

'Please, Madame, don't worry. I will go and look for her straight away. I'm sure there will be a simple explanation.'

'I will go upstairs and have a look round, in case she has come back without us realising. I will see if she has taken her phone with her.'

'Ok, Madame. Hopefully, I will be back shortly with Rosalinde.'

Didier went out through the side door and followed the path that Rosalinde had taken that afternoon. He walked to the lake and turned left to follow the path round. He could see that someone had recently walked that way, because the grass was quite long in places and it had been flattened by footsteps.

He was almost all the way around the lake when he came to the big, old oak tree. Under the tree there was a large patch of flattened grass; it looked as if someone had been rolling around in the grass. Didier thought it could have ended up like that after a struggle. 'Oh my God,' he thought. 'What if something has happened to Rosalinde?' He looked closer, trying to see if there was anything to give him a clue about what had taken place here. He searched on his hands and knees, parting the long grasses with his bare hands.

Then, out of the corner of his eye, he saw something: it was a fine, gold necklace, the clasp broken, as if it had been torn off in a struggle. He searched again through the grass and found a small, gold locket.

Didier took a deep breath. He had seen this necklace before around Rosalinde's neck. He slumped back on his bottom, on the damp grass. His breathing was rapid and he felt very shaky. What on earth had happened here? He looked around, scanning the whole area from where he sat, but he couldn't see anything else. He sat for a moment, trying to grasp the situation. He got up slowly. 'Go steady,' he told himself. 'If something has happened to Rosalinde, you need to be careful. You don't want to fall or run into something.'

He knew he must get back to Madame and, as he turned to head home, he saw something hidden near the old oak tree, in the grass: a roll of duct tape and a knife. 'Oh, God!' he said out loud, and then promptly looked around himself, but there was nobody there.

Didier knew he must not touch the knife or the duct tape, but he didn't want to leave it where it was, in case the person or persons that had used it came back. He knew he must get back to the château and tell Madame, so she could call the police. He decided to leave the knife and tape and head back as quickly as possible. He had already picked up the locket and chain, so he carefully wrapped them in his handkerchief and put them in his pocket.

Meanwhile, back at the château, Mathilde had decided to try ringing Rosalinde on her mobile, but all she kept getting was the answerphone service. She had been up to Rosalinde's room to see if she had returned and fallen asleep on the bed, but there was no sign of her. Mathilde's anxiety levels were beginning to rise, which was not good for her, as she had a mild heart condition that was made worse by stress.

Just as she got back downstairs, the telephone rang. 'Oh,' thought Mathilde, 'that must be Rosalinde now. Thank goodness for that!' She crossed the hallway to the telephone and quickly picked it up before it stopped ringing. 'Bonsoir,' said Mathilde.

'Bonsoir, Madame,' said a male voice, which sounded very odd, almost as if it were coming from a tunnel.

Mathilde was disappointed that it was not Rosalinde on the phone and was a little taken aback, as she was so sure it would be her on the phone.

'Madame, I expect you are wondering what has happened to your granddaughter. I have her – she is my hostage. Do not go to the police or attempt to look for her yourself. Wait until you hear from me with further instructions.'

Then the phone went dead.

Mathilde froze. She could not believe it was true. How and why had this happened? Just at that moment, Didier came crashing into the hallway. Mathilde was still clutching the phone in her hand. They looked at each other in horror, both knowing something was wrong.

'Something has happened to Rosalinde, Madame. I have found her locket broken by the old oak – and Madame – I don't know how to tell you this – but I found some duct tape and a knife.'

'Didier, I – I – I know. Oh my God!' Mathilde dropped into the chair that Didier quickly placed behind her. She was breathing rapidly and her heart was beating wildly.

'Who was on the phone, Madame?'

Mathilde looked across at Didier. He was her servant, but he had been with her for so long she knew she could trust him. 'The answer is I don't know who was on the phone, but...' She paused to take a breath. '...he has got Rosalinde!'

'What do you mean he has got Rosalinde? Surely we should be ringing the police.' Didier moved to pick up the telephone.

'NO!' shouted Mathilde. 'Don't ring them. He specifically said not to.'

'We can't just sit here doing nothing – we must get some help.' Mathilde was shaking violently and holding a handkerchief to her face. Didier realised she was crying.

'He is going to ring back. We must do as he says and not attempt to look for her or involve the police,' she managed to say, before breaking into sobs.

Didier got another chair and sat beside Mathilde. They sat side by side in silence. Didier was worried about Mathilde; she was not in the best of health and a shock like this could quite possibly bring on a heart attack. She was not looking good. He reached over and took her hand in his. He rubbed her hand and looked her in the eyes and said, 'We will get through this. It will be ok. I'm here for you and we must be strong.'

Mathilde heaved a great big sigh and leaned into Didier. She was so grateful she had him to rely on and to share this burden with.

'Now I am going to go to the kitchen and make us some tea and sandwiches. We must keep our strength up. We do not know how long it will be before the kidnapper rings back – this could be a very long night.'

'Thank you, Didier. I don't think I could get through this without you.' Didier squeezed her hand and gave her a quick hug, which took Mathilde by surprise, but was nonetheless welcome.

'If the telephone rings, I will come straight back,' he said. Then he put a rug over her knees and made his way to the kitchen to make their supper.

They ate and drank in silence, Mathilde hardly taking her eyes off the telephone, the atmosphere heavy and expectant. Three hours had passed and still no phone call. It was almost midnight. Mathilde was struggling to keep her eyes open; Didier had long given up the struggle and was quietly snoring in his chair. Mathilde was debating whether to go to bed or stay up. She didn't think she would be able to sleep if she got up and went to bed, but at least her old bones would be more comfortable.

'Didier,' she called softly.

He slowly stirred, and then remembered the situation, rapidly coming to. 'Madame, has something happened? I'm sorry – I must have dropped off to sleep.'

'No, no, nothing yet. Although I don't think I will sleep, I'm going to lie down. It will be more comfortable.'

'Yes, Madame. It is very late. I don't think we will hear anything tonight.' Didier was cross with himself for falling asleep when Mathilde needed him.

Mathilde struggled to her feet and pulled her shawl tighter around her shoulders. She shivered; the evening had turned colder, and it had started to rain. 'Poor Rosalinde,' she thought. 'Wherever she is, I hope she's warm and comfortable.' As she crossed the room and reached for the door handle, the telephone rang. Didier looked up at her and for a moment she faltered. Then she was across the room in a flash and snatched up the phone.

At the other end of the phone, Guy had disguised his voice. 'Good evening, Madame La Roche.'

Chapter Twelve.

Rosalinde woke up with a start. Her head hurt and she felt constricted, but she couldn't understand why. Then she tried to take a deep breath and realised her mouth was covered. 'Oh my God!' She remembered what had happened: the man had attacked her and then everything had gone black.

She tried to move, and noticed she was bound up with some kind of rope. Where the hell was she? She moved her head and the pain made her feel sick. All her senses were on high alert and she began to panic.

She willed herself to calm down, to try and make out where she was, but it was dark and very difficult to move. Rosalinde ached all over and suddenly felt very cold; she must be in shock, as she had been injured. She really needed to pee. 'Oh my God! What the hell am I going to do?' She couldn't shout for help; her mouth was covered in duct tape. She was desperate for someone to come, so she could pee. On the other hand, what the hell were they going to do to her if they did come?

It was at this point that she broke down and started to sob. Her body shook from head to toe and the tears poured down her cheeks, her ribs heaving with great big, racking sobs. When she realised crying was making it harder to breathe, she tried to calm down. She stopped crying and breathed in slowly through her nose, calming her body down slowly. Gradually, the shaking began to slow down, and she stopped sobbing.

'Getting in a state is not going to help,' she told herself, so she began to assess the situation. It was too dark to see anything; she tried to see if there was even the smallest chink of light, but there was nothing. Next, she listened. At first, she couldn't hear anything and then, as if it was quite far away, she could hear cows softly mooing. That meant she must be in the countryside somewhere. If only she hadn't blacked out when she hit her head! She just could not remember how she ended up here.

Then she began to sniff. It was musty and old smelling, but not damp, so she must be above ground, she decided. And there was something else: straw or hay. Yes, that was it, but it didn't smell of fresh hay; it was old and dusty. She was getting somewhere now. Her hands were tied behind her back, palms facing the floor. Rosalinde felt the floor beneath her; it felt like old, rough, wooden floorboards. So she must be in a farm building somewhere, she concluded, but the question was, where?

Her legs were bound together with rope, but she managed to roll onto her side and then onto her front. Her arm came into contact with the stone wall. She pushed her whole body up against the wall; all she could feel were the individual stones. With all her might she then rolled back onto her side, onto her back and over onto her other side, where she encountered another stone wall.

'Ok,' she thought. 'I'm in a fairly small space.' Again, all she could feel were the stones in the wall. After all this exertion, she was exhausted. She rolled back onto her front and just lay there, not sure how much longer she could hang on before she wet herself. She tried to lift her legs to see how high the space was, but the rope was too heavy; she could only lift them halfway up. 'Oh, God!' she thought. 'Why am I here? And what the hell is going to happen to me?' She could feel the panic rising, but then she heard a noise.

She lay still, every muscle straining and tense, trying to listen, in case she heard anything. Then she heard it again: footsteps. Someone was coming. Her heart started pounding and her breathing became agitated. She could hear footsteps running and it sounded as if they were coming up a staircase. Her mind was whirling, trying to figure out where she could be, but before she had time for any more thoughts, she could hear something large being moved. Someone was sliding something along the floor, and then a key turned in the lock.

'This is it,' she thought. 'I am going to come face to face with whoever has done this to me.' The door started to open, scraping the floor as it was pulled back, and the light began to spill into the area where she was lying. Rosalinde wanted to look, but was so scared that she closed her eyes and remained as still as she could.

It was very late at night. Guy had had to sneak out of the flat he shared with Therese. He knew he could not leave Rosalinde all night without checking on her. He had driven to the old barn and made sure he had covered his face, before going in to see her.

'I know you are awake and I'm sure you must need to pee, so I am going to untie you and let you use a bucket. Don't attempt to escape – I will use force if I have to. I have done it once and will do it again.'

Rosalinde opened her eyes. The light was very dim, and she could not see much, but she could make out the size of the man in front of her. He was big and dressed in black, with a mask covering his face. As he pulled her from what she could now see was some kind of cupboard, she felt so weak that there was no way she could fight him or try to escape. Instead, she tried to look around and ascertain her whereabouts. Guy untied her hands and led her over to a bucket. At least he had the decency to turn away as she relieved herself. She quickly pulled her jeans back up, all the time looking around, trying to get her bearings. She couldn't speak to him, as he hadn't removed the duct tape from her mouth. Now she had peed, she realised she was desperately thirsty and hoped he had brought her something to drink. She mimed drinking at him, and he pulled her over to a bale of straw and sat her down.

'Yes, I have brought you food and drink, but I am going to have to untape your mouth. Do not scream or I will hit you – not that anyone will be able to hear you anyway.' Guy slowly removed the tape from Rosalinde's mouth, which was pretty painful, but she did not let him see that it hurt. 'Ok, I have some water and bread and cheese for you. If you sit quietly and eat it, I will come again in the morning with more food, but any tricks and I will leave you alone.'

Rosalinde was terrified. She reached out for the water, her hand shaking so badly she spilled most of it before it got to her mouth. She wanted to ask him what this was all about but was scared, so just accepted the food and water. She could tell she was in a barn, yet had no idea where the barn was. It could be one of Mathilde's barns. As she had not been in all of the outbuildings, though, she didn't recognise it.

'Good. You have behaved very well, so I will come back in the morning. Do you want to use the bucket again before I go?'

'Yes,' she nodded.

Her mind was working overtime, trying to think of how she could escape. There was no way out, not at this moment; she would have to bide her time. Now she had relieved herself and she had eaten and drunk and the man had not attacked her, she should have felt slightly calmer, but somehow she didn't.

'He must need me alive,' she decided. 'Otherwise, why would he be feeding me and keeping me locked up? If he was going to kill me, he would have done it by now.' This thought gave her some comfort. But why? Why was he holding her captive? She wasn't worth anything. Then a thought came into her head: Mathilde! What if he had kidnapped her to get at Mathilde? 'Oh, God, I hope she is alright.'

'Ok, it's time for you to go back in the cupboard.'

'No, please don't put me there! It's so dark and uncomfortable.'

He looked at her with dark, menacing eyes and said, 'You will do as I say – you have no choice.'

He quickly taped up her mouth and tied her up again with the heavy rope, then dragged her back into the cupboard. She was shaking and crying, but he completely ignored her and just went about his business, as if it was an everyday occurrence. The door was slammed shut and she could hear padlocks being locked and then what sounded like a bale of straw being dragged across the floor. 'He's hiding the cupboard door,' she thought. Her ears strained, trying to hear the smallest sound; she heard him cross the floor and descend some stairs and then a door quietly closing.

Then silence. Her ears were desperately trying to pick up any sound, but there was nothing but silence. Rosalinde could feel the anxiety building in her again. She willed herself not to cry, but she failed. Tears rolled down her cheeks as she wept. She tried not to give way to full blown sobbing, as she knew she wouldn't be able to breathe or wipe the tears away.

Gradually, the crying stopped, and she began to calm down. Maybe she could wriggle and loosen the rope that was binding her hands. Rosalinde struggled and twisted and turned, but the ropes were too tight. Eventually, she gave up, exhausted. A wave of despondency came over her, as she realised there was no escape.

A thought came into her head: Mathilde must have noticed she was missing by now and hopefully would have raised the alarm. Surely, she would have phoned the police and they would be out looking for her. She could only hope that they would find her before long, but for now, she faced a long, uncomfortable night.

Rosalinde tried not to think of what might happen to her in the morning when the man came back. She decided to get some sleep, to try and regain some of her strength. Maybe she could try bargaining with him and he might let her go, or she could try to escape. For now, she would try to sleep. It was very uncomfortable, but she was exhausted from crying and, thankfully, she could hardly keep her eyes open.

Just as she drifted off to sleep, Rosalinde could faintly hear the sound of bells chiming on the church clock. If only she knew which church. Every village in France had a church with bells that tolled the hours. Ten o'clock, the bells chimed. She must try to listen and keep track of the time. She immediately fell asleep.

Chapter Thirteen.

Mathilde woke up with a start. The events of the night before came back in an instant; she felt anxious and extremely concerned for Rosalinde. She gazed at her bedside clock: six a.m. Well, at least she had managed to get some sleep. There was a quiet knock on the door, after which it opened very slowly: Didier bringing her morning coffee, as he had done for many years.

Mathilde sat up in bed, as he placed the tray on the bedside table. She glanced at him and saw that he had not slept.

'Bonjour, Madame. Did you manage to get any sleep?' he asked.

'Bonjour, Didier. Yes, a little. You look as if you haven't slept at all.'

'No, Madame, I confess I have not. My head was spinning trying to think where Miss Rosalinde could be?'

'Yes, I can understand that. Do you think we should try and look for her on the estate? After all, there are so many old buildings – she could be hidden in any one of them.'

Didier had thought of this already, but he didn't say so. The fact was she could be anywhere, right under their noses or miles away. Although he wanted to go and search for Rosalinde, he was concerned about the kidnapper finding out and then taking it out on her and maybe harming her. 'Madame, my only concern is if we are seen to be searching by the kidnapper, he may harm Miss Rosalinde.'

'But Didier, I cannot just sit here and do nothing.'

Didier could see she was starting to get upset again, so he handed her the coffee cup and said, 'Madame, please drink this and then get up. I will go and prepare your breakfast, as you must keep your strength up.' He turned and left the room before she could argue.

Mathilde sighed. She knew Didier was right. She got up and, as quickly as an old lady could, she washed and dressed and then went downstairs to the dining room. As she sat down at the dining room table, the telephone rang. She leapt to her feet, but Didier beat her to it.

'Bonjour, le Château La Roche.'

'Bonjour.' Instantly, Didier knew it was the kidnapper. 'May I speak to Madame La Roche?'

'Yes. One moment, please.' Didier carried the phone over to Mathilde. They looked into each other's eyes and Didier mouthed 'It's him' to Mathilde.

She took a deep breath and answered in as calm and dignified a manner as she could. 'Madame La Roche speaking.'

'Bonjour, Madame. I hope you have not spoken to the police or anyone else.'

'No, I have not. Please tell me that my granddaughter is safe and being well cared for.'

'Yes, she is fine.'

'I would like proof of that, before I agree to any of your demands.'

'I will bring you proof, but I have not told you my demands yet and you would do well to remember that I am in charge of this situation.'

Mathilde drew in a large breath to steady herself. 'Yes, I understand,' she said meekly.

'Now, let's get down to business. You value your granddaughter and so I assume you are willing to pay for her safe return.'

'Of course I am!' Mathilde could feel the anger rising inside her, but she quickly swallowed it down, knowing it would only antagonize him if she made an angry retort.

'Good.'

Guy was enjoying this: having power over someone, a person he considered to be above him. Now she was going to have to bow and scrape to him, not the other way around. His chest swelled; he felt big and important. He had the upper hand. 'I want you to listen very carefully to what I am going to say. You will not interrupt me or make any comment until I have finished. Do you understand?'

Mathilde was shaking from head to foot. Her heart was beating wildly but she managed to whisper, 'I understand.'

Didier silently pulled up a chair and came to sit next to Mathilde. He reached out and took her free hand in his, holding it gently but firmly. He looked directly into Mathilde's eyes, letting her know he was truly there for her. In return, she nodded to him: a silent confirmation that she knew what he was implying.

'Right, I shall begin. Madame, I have heard the rumours that you have a fortune hidden in your château. You live like a pauper, but everyone around here knows there are jewels hidden somewhere in that great, big château. Why you live like a pauper is your own business, and why you are hanging onto this hidden fortune is beyond me. Anyway, my point is that I want your fortune – the jewels. It is time for you to come up with the goods, as it were. Now, I will be fair. I will give you forty-eight hours, and then I want the jewels in whatever form they take.'

Mathilde was horrified. Yes, of course she had heard the rumours, too, about the lost jewels, but she did not know their whereabouts. What on earth was she going to do?

'I will contact you in twenty-four hours, to see how you are getting on. I will tell you where to deliver the jewels and where you will find your granddaughter, of course.'

'But Monsieur, I don't know where they are. It is an impossible task!' Mathilde was talking to thin air. Guy had rung off before he had heard a single word.

'Oh, Didier, what are we going to do? I have no idea about these so-called jewels. I have heard the stories over the years like everyone else, but I thought they were just that.'

'Madame, I have also heard the rumours, but never believed them to be true.'

'I really don't know what to do. Even if it was true, where would we start to look?'

'Madame, I think we should go to the police. The situation is very serious, and we have no way of resolving it.'

'No, Didier! He specifically said not to. I'm too scared of the consequences for Rosalinde if we do that. I agree we do need help, though.'

As they sat there, momentarily lost in their thoughts, they heard a car engine coming up the drive. Mathilde looked at Didier and sighed. 'Oh, no! It's that electric man. He has come to start work. What shall we do?' asked Mathilde.

'I think we must let him work. We must carry on as normal, in case we are being watched, Madame.'

'Yes, of course, but what are we going to do about looking for these so-called jewels. I don't even know if they exist.'

Mathilde was feeling very overcome and Didier was getting concerned for her welfare. She had begun to look very pale and was taking huge, gasping breaths. 'Madame, please calm yourself. You will not help Miss Rosalinde if you become ill.'

'Ok, I know. Didier, please could you make me some fresh coffee and go and tell the electric man he must not work in the house today. I really can't face seeing him. Tell him I'm not well and ask him to work outside.'

'Yes, Madame. Of course.'

Didier went straight to the kitchen and put the coffee on to brew. Then he went outside to where Guy's van was parked. 'Bonjour, Monsieur. Please could you not come into the house today, as Madame is unwell. Perhaps you have something you can be doing outside instead.'

'Yes, that's fine. I can work in the old stables.'

Guy was nervous. He had decided he must still turn up for work, as it would look very suspicious if he didn't. He collected his tools from the van and made his way over to the stables – not that there were any horses in them or had been for many years. So, the old lady was feeling ill. 'I bet she is,' he thought to himself. Still, the barn was a good spot to keep an eye on them, in case they decided to call in some outside help. From the stables, he could sneak around the back to the old barn and check on Rosalinde without being seen from the house.

Mathilde sat hunched in her armchair. Again and again, in her mind she went over what the kidnapper had said to her. Of course, she had heard about the jewels over the years, but she had always believed it to be rumours. She kept turning it over and over in her mind. What on earth was she going to do? Mathilde La Roche had always been a strong woman; she was known for it. Firm but fair was how the locals saw her, but if they could see her now, they would have a very different opinion. She felt old, as if she had shrivelled up into a helpless geriatric, because of the present situation.

She thought about the sheer size of the château. It was vast – at least fifty rooms – and then there were all the outbuildings. Even if they started to search, it would take months. She had not entered some of the rooms for years. They were still full of furniture, most of them covered with dust sheets. Mathilde tried to remember the stories her mother-in-law had told her when she came to the château as a young bride, over sixty years ago. She wished she had listened now, but as a young, happy newlywed, she hadn't had a lot of time for the older woman.

However, remnants of the story were coming back to her. She pictured herself sitting in her mother-in-law's sitting room on the second floor. They were having coffee and Marie-France had decided that Mathilde needed to learn a little of the château's history.

'Now, Mathilde, I don't know what you have heard about the château in the past, but I think it's only right that you should learn some of the history of the place, as one day you and my son will be in charge.'

'Thank you, Madame.' Young Mathilde knew she must be courteous, even though she would rather sit in the garden reading her latest fashion magazine, containing wonderful photographs of Christian Dior's latest creations. It seemed a long way off in the future that she would be responsible for the château.

Suddenly, it came back to her: the story of the jewels. Now, what was it? Yes – yes, that was it – a girl called Sophie...

It was the night when the château was broken into. The Comte and Comtesse had fled earlier that morning, taking their children, but there wasn't time to gather any possessions. The Comtesse's cousin, who was governess to the children, had also been left behind. The story went that the villagers had stormed the house and were going to burn it to the ground, until they had discovered the Comte's wine cellar. They all ended up blind drunk, passing out before a flame was lit. The next morning, they all woke up with sore heads, but the desire to torch the château had gone. Instead, they stole various items from the château and went home. It was said that they went looking for the Comtesse's jewellery, only to find someone had beaten them to it. At the time everyone assumed it was Sophie, the governess, who had taken the jewellery. The Comte and his family returned to the château several years later, but the jewellery and Sophie were never seen again.

'Oh my God!' thought Mathilde. 'That was over two hundred years ago.' She was sure people had searched over the intervening years; she had herself as a young woman. All to no avail. Now, this mad man had her granddaughter were hidden somewhere, on the pretext that there was some loot hidden in the château.

Mathilde looked at her watch as it was approaching midday, almost forty-eight hours since anyone had seen Rosalinde. The more she thought about the situation, the more panicked she became. She had no idea if these so-called jewels even existed. Perhaps Didier was right – they should contact the police – but what if the kidnapper harmed Rosalinde on finding out they had called in help? She would never forgive herself.

She rang the bell for Didier. She was in turmoil: half of her said they must get help, but the other half was terrified. Didier was taking his time. Where was he, for goodness' sake? She rang the bell again.

Didier could hear Madame ringing the bell, but he had taken it upon himself to start a search for the jewels. He was in the attic, as he had decided to start at the top and work his way down. The main problem was he didn't know what he was looking for. When Madame rang for a second time, he decided he had better answer her; otherwise she would only get even more upset. As he made his way downstairs, he thought about his futile search, deeming it an impossible task. He must convince Madame to call the police. Miss Rosalinde had been gone over twenty-four hours already. They had no idea if what they were searching for even existed anymore.

Didier entered Madame's sitting room. He looked across the room at her: she looked so frail and had visibly aged in the last two days.

'You rang, Madame?'

'Yes, Didier. What took you so long? I had to ring twice!'

'I'm sorry, Madame. I was searching the attic. I just thought we must start somewhere.'

'Yes, well, I have been thinking about what you said – about getting some help – and I have decided you are right.'

'Very good, Madame. Shall I call the police?'

'No, Didier. I am very worried about the kidnapper finding out that we are asking for help, so I am going to call my old friend, Monsieur Hubert. As you know, he is a retired police inspector.'

'That is a very good idea, Madame, but what if the kidnapper has bugged the telephone?'

'Oh, Didier, I hadn't thought of that. What shall we do?'

'Don't worry, Madame – I have an idea. Miss Rosalinde has a mobile phone – it is in her room. We could use that.'

'Yes, brilliant, Didier. Quickly go and get it and we will ring him straight away.'

As he left the room, Mathilde went to her writing desk and took out her battered address book. She quickly looked up M. Hubert's number. She was still wondering if they were doing the right thing.

Didier came back, puffing and panting with exertion. 'Now, Madame, if you read out the numbers, I will punch them into the phone.'

Mathilde read out the numbers and Didier could hear the dialling tone, so he handed the phone over to Mathilde.

'Bonjour,' said Monsieur Hubert.

'Bonjour, Maxim, it's Mathilde La Roche.'

'Mathilde, how lovely to hear from you. We haven't met for a long time. How are you, my dear?'

'Well – oh, I don't know where to start. I have got a very serious problem and I'm sorry to call you out of the blue like this, but I didn't know who else to call.'

'Right, ok. Let's start at the beginning then.'

Mathilde took a deep breath and then told him the whole story, starting with the fact that she had found her long lost granddaughter.

At the end of Mathilde's long story, Maxim Hubert let out a long sigh. 'You indeed have a very big problem, Madame, which needs very careful handling. I understand your reluctance to involve the police, but I can see no other way of resolving the situation.'

'Maxim, I have only just found my granddaughter. I do not wish to lose her, and I am terrified that is what is going to happen.'

'Of course. I can see your point of view, but Mathilde, you cannot do this alone. When is the kidnapper going to contact you again?'

'This evening, but I have no idea what I shall say to him when he asks me about the jewels.'

'Ok. I have some friends in the police, who I can rely on to be discreet. We can put a tap on the line and listen in from the station. Nobody will know or see what is being done covertly. Now, I will go and set things up, as we don't have a lot of time. If you are contacted by him, ring me straight away. Otherwise, try not to use the telephone and I will be in touch as soon as possible.'

He rang off. Mathilde was left clutching the phone in her hand. Her stomach was in knots and she was still wondering if she had done the right thing.

Chapter Fourteen.

After Guy had spoken to the butler, Didier, he felt quite confident that they had not told anybody about the kidnapping and that they did not suspect him. However, he was going to have to be very careful not to leave a trail behind him.

He made his way over to the old barn, where he was holding Rosalinde hostage. He wanted to check on her, give her some food and let her use the bucket again. He was careful to put his mask on before seeing her. He was only thinking of the outcome and getting his hands on the jewels. He really wasn't bothered if Rosalinde was suffering; it was just a means to an end. He made his way up the stairs and moved all the bales of straw once again. As he unlocked the door and looked in through the opening, he could see Rosalinde lying on her side with her back to him. He grabbed hold of the rope that was tied around her back and pulled her towards the open doorway. As he did this, he pulled her over onto her back. She just lay there, looking up at him. All the fight had gone out of her; it was as if she had given up. This shocked Guy. He thought she was a fighter and had been expecting trouble from her. Instead, she lay there like a rag doll.

'Do you want to eat?' he asked her.

No reply.

'Do you want to use the bucket?'

Again, no reply. Was she playing a game with him? He couldn't tell.

'Ok, I'm going to untie you and sit you up on a bale of straw. Don't try anything, because you will regret it.'

She looked up into his eyes, her face a blank mask – no fear, just blank. It completely unnerved him. He started to think she must have hit her head when she fell and sustained an injury. Guy checked Rosalinde's head for a wound or a lump, but all looked fine. He removed the tape from her mouth and then opened a bottle of water and held it to her lips. She started to drink, swallowing great, big gulps. She then began to come back to life. He could see she was dehydrated and quite weak; she had been crying and had worn herself out.

'Please, please can I have something to eat?'

He had no need to worry about her fighting him; she was so weak she couldn't even stand up. He gave her some bread and an apple. Whilst she was eating it, he thought about the situation. He hoped the old woman came up with the goods quickly, because he wouldn't be able to keep her like this for much longer. He didn't want to have to dispose of a body. She finished eating and used the bucket. He then sat her back on a bale of straw, took out his phone, and took a picture of her.

'What are you doing that for?' Rosalinde asked in a weak voice.

'I need proof that you are alive.'

Rosalinde shook with horror. This made the situation suddenly more terrifying. She now realized he must be holding her for some sort of ransom. She slumped down and hunched over, her mind reeling at what he had just said.

When it came to tying her up again and putting her back into the cupboard, she didn't put up a fight. Guy found this more difficult than if she had fought him.

Rosalinde was struggling. She felt weak; most of the previous night she had been in tears. She knew she must not give up, but somehow she had lost the will to fight. There was no point in fighting the man when he came to give her food and water. At least she didn't feel hungry and thirsty anymore, but she would like a cup of hot coffee – she was so cold. That wasn't coming anytime soon. She tried to think about where she might be and how she could escape. Maybe when he untied her to use the bucket next time she could get away. The trouble was she ached all over and was so stiff from lying on a hard floor.

She looked around her: in the dark she could just make out that the space was tiny. Even if she could stand up, there wasn't enough height to do so. 'I must try to move,' she thought. She rolled onto her side and back again, then onto her other side and then onto her front. The exertion made her sweat, but it gave her some satisfaction in that she could do it. She rested for a minute and then did it again. She repeated this exercise five more times, until she was exhausted. At least she was doing something; she had begun to fight. For whatever reason this man was holding her, she was not going to give up.

Rosalinde trusted Mathilde must know that she was missing and was organising a search for her. If only JJ was here! She hoped he would search for her, too. Oh, she almost wished she hadn't thought about him; it brought up so many feelings and she started to well up inside. Panic began inside of her and she started to cry again.

Then she suddenly stopped. 'No, I will not cry,' she told herself. 'I must remain strong. I will get through this and JJ and I will be together.' Rosalinde drifted off to sleep, thinking about JJ and their future together. At least it gave her some comfort.

Guy was downstairs in the barn. He had taken his tools out of the van and spread them around, so it looked like he was working. He was worried Rosalinde didn't look good. What if she died or the old woman didn't come up with anything? What would he do with Rosalinde then? He hadn't thought this through. Still, he would send the picture to the old woman and then he would have to get rid of the phone straight away, just in case she had called in some help. How on earth was he going to send this photo? He didn't know if the old woman had a mobile phone. He didn't want to go home and print it from his computer, in case Therese saw it and started asking questions. The only way was to go to an internet café and print it off there, being very careful that nobody saw what he was up to. Guy looked at his watch: as it was approaching lunchtime, he would go to the café now and print off the photo, and then he could ditch the phone at the same time.

Guy looked through the window of the internet café. Luckily there was only a young girl in there, using one of the terminals. He entered and made his way to the far right hand corner. He quickly connected the phone using the lead that was provided and followed the instructions on the screen. The whole time he was doing this he had one eye on the screen and one on the rest of the café, praying that no one would come over to talk to him. After what seemed like an age, the printer whirred into life and the photo shunted out onto the tray. He grabbed it up and stuffed it into the inside pocket of his jacket. Inside, his heart was racing, but he told himself to slow down; the last thing he needed was to draw attention to himself. He went over to the counter and paid for the time he had used and then left as calmly as he could.

He would return to the château and leave the photo in the post box at the end of the drive. Subsequently, he would phone Madame to tell her where to find it, and then ditch the phone in the lake on the way back to the barn.

He was quite pleased with himself. So far, nobody seemed at all suspicious. Therese was happy at home, and the old woman and the butler didn't have any idea that he was the kidnapper. However, he still felt very uneasy about the state of Rosalinde.

He took out the phone and dialled the château's number.

'Bonjour.' A weary sounding Mathilde La Roche answered the phone.

'Bonjour, Madame. You will find the proof that your granddaughter is alive in the post box. Now, have you found what I want?'

'No, Monsieur. I need more time. The rumours of the jewels are, as far as I know, just rumours.'

'Please be assured, Madame, that I will not wait much longer. Your granddaughter is in danger.'

Guy then pressed the button to end the call. He drove past the lake and, having switched off the phone, he casually threw it out of the window into the lake.

Mathilde turned to Didier. 'In the post box, he says there is proof that Rosalinde is alive.'

'I will go there now, Madame.'

Didier left the room and quickly made his way to the post box on the old golf cart that he used to get around the estate. Mathilde sat in her chair, Guy's words ringing in her ears. After all these years of being alone, she finally had some family to love, but it was no sooner here than gone. The possibility of losing Rosalinde was unbearable; it would be like losing Louis all over again.

Didier found the photograph in the post box in a torn brown envelope. He carefully removed it, wearing gloves just in case fingerprints were on the envelope. As soon as he arrived back at the château, he passed the photo over to Mathilde, making her hold it with a handkerchief.

Mathilde silently started to cry as she looked at the photo. Rosalinde looked dreadful. Her hair was matted, and she looked grey and ill – not the happy, bright young woman Mathilde had met only a few days before.

'Oh, Didier, what on earth are we going to do?' she cried.

'Madame, we must tell Monsieur Hubert straight away.'

'But what if the kidnapper is watching us?'

'Madame, I will ring Monsieur Hubert on Miss Rosalinde's mobile and arrange to meet him. I can make it look as if I am going grocery shopping.'

'Didier, you are a genius! Where on earth did you get such an idea? I can see I'm going to have to watch you.'

Didier felt a slight relief that she was able to make a joke, considering the situation. 'Madame, I like to watch crime dramas on TV – that's all.'

He walked over to the coffee table, picked up Rosalinde's phone, and dialled Hubert's number. The phone was answered on the second ring.

'Bonjour?'

'Bonjour, Monsieur. It is Didier, Madame La Roche's butler, here.'

'Yes, Didier, how can I help?' Hubert was always straight to the point.

'We have received a photograph of Rosalinde from the kidnapper.'

'Good. How does she look? And be careful how you answer me, Didier, as I presume Madame is listening.'

Didier took a deep breath and quickly gathered his thoughts. 'She is alive, Monsieur, and looks reasonable,' he replied, although he really thought she looked dreadful.

Hubert was no fool; he could tell the butler was being cagey, for the sake of Madame La Roche. 'Can you see anything in the background of the photo that could indicate where it was taken, Didier?'

Didier looked at the photo again. It was very dark. All he could see was Rosalinde's wan face looking back at him; the background was all in darkness. 'No, Monsieur – it is too dark.' He turned his back to Mathilde and whispered into the phone, 'Please, Monsieur, what shall we do?'

Hubert ran his hand over his chin and sighed; there was only one thing they could do. 'We are going to have to go to the police, my friend – we have no choice. I am very concerned for the young lady, as well as the health of my friend, Madame, not to mention the strain it is putting on you. You are not a young man, Didier, and it is too much for you to deal with.'

'Yes, I agree with you. Shall I telephone them, or will you?' Didier could hear Mathilde sobbing behind him; he would worry about that in a minute.

'I will phone them, Didier. I will speak to an old colleague of mine, so that we can keep this as quiet as possible.'

'Very good, sir. I will ring off so you can get on with it then. Please can you keep us informed of any developments?'

'Of course. Oh, and Didier, please tell Madame to try not to worry. Most of these cases have a good outcome.'

Didier ended the call and turned around to face Mathilde. She looked up at him with tears in her eyes. 'Well, what is going to happen now?'

'He is going to inform the police and he will keep us posted. He told me to tell you not to worry too much as, usually, these cases have a good outcome.' Didier decided not to elaborate.

'How can I not worry? That man has my only Grandchild!'

'Yes, I know, Madame. He is only thinking of your health. He will keep us informed of any developments. Now, I'm going to insist that you eat something and then have a lie down. If there is any news, I will tell you straight away.'

Chapter Fifteen.

Rosalinde willed herself awake. 'I must be strong,' she told herself. She felt so weak, but she made herself roll to her side and back three times, just to try and keep her muscles working. It was dark in the cupboard and cold, but she knew she must fight to keep going and get her strength back.

When the kidnapper had let her out to use the bucket, she had been acting. She did feel weak and her head still hurt from the fall, but she was not as bad as she had made out. She had been secretly looking around and she could tell she was in one of the château's old outbuildings. If only she could free herself from the ropes, she could try to escape, but they were tied so tightly that, try as she might, she could not make them budge.

Her fighting spirit had come back, and she was determined she was going to survive this ordeal. She just had to think of a way. Her mind was all over the place, but she knew her best chance would be when the kidnapper came to feed her and let her use the bucket to relieve herself, because he had no choice but to untie her then. Rosalinde knew he came early in the morning and again at night. If she tried to escape, her best bet would be at night; it would be easier to hide from him in the dark. He had already been this morning and had taken a photo of her, presumably to show Mathilde that she was still alive.

Rosalinde wondered how Mathilde was and whether she had spoken to her mother. Oh, God! Everyone would be worrying about her and they wouldn't have a clue where she was. This thought made her even more determined to get free. She decided to wait until tomorrow evening to try to escape, mainly because she thought she might feel stronger by then. It would also give her a chance to look around at her surroundings a couple more times, so she could get her bearings. For now, she decided to sleep. The old Rosalinde was coming back and was not going to be beaten.

Jean-Jacques sped up the drive to Château La Roche; he couldn't wait to see Rosalinde again. He had only been gone a few days, but it felt like ages since he had seen her. He had decided not to ring ahead to tell her he was on his way back. He thought it would be more romantic to just turn up and surprise her. His mother was going to be fine; the doctors had her medication under control and his sisters, Violette and Beatrice, were staying with her for the next couple of weeks. His only worry was that Rosalinde might have changed her mind about him. If that was the case, he would have to try and convince her otherwise. He did wonder why Rosalinde was staying at the château, but then thought it was probably easier than to keep driving backward and forwards to town. And if the old lady didn't mind, why not? He hoped Rosalinde had nearly finished photographing the château, because then they could spend some time together and get to know each other a little better.

As he pulled up in front of the château, he took in its beauty. In the sunlight, it looked magnificent, the grey slates on the turrets shining like silver and the beautiful pink stone glowing beneath them. He glanced at his watch: it was lunchtime. Perfect! He thought Rosalinde should be stopping for lunch. Maybe he could whisk her away for a couple of hours to a quiet, little restaurant. He grabbed the bunch of flowers lying on the passenger seat and leapt from the car, ran up the steps to the front door, and rang the bell. He was hoping if the butler opened the door, he could tell him where Rosalinde was in the château, so he could go and surprise her. The door opened and Didier stood in front of him. As JJ looked at him, he instantly knew something was wrong. The butler had visibly aged since JJ had been away. He looked like a different person; his face looked drawn and grey, like the worries of the world were on his shoulders.

'Bonjour, Didier.'

'Bonjour, Monsieur Jean-Jacques. Please come in.'

JJ quickly entered the hallway and said to Didier, 'Has something happened since I've been away? If you don't mind me saying, you don't look like your usual self.'

'Oh, Jean-Jacques, I don't know where to start!'

JJ was beginning to get very worried; he could see Didier was crumbling in front of him.

'Please come into the salon. Madame is in there and we can explain what is going on.'

'But where is Rosalinde?' he asked, still holding the flowers.

'Oh, sir, so much has happened in such a short time. If you will just come with me, we will explain.'

JJ could feel the atmosphere change around him as he walked into the salon. Mathilde looked as if she had shrunk and aged about ten years. What on earth had happened to make them go downhill so fast, he wondered. He had only been gone a few days!

'Bonjour, Jean-Jacques. Thank goodness you have returned,' said Mathilde, trying to put on a brave face.

'Bonjour, Madame. Please tell me what is going on. Clearly something bad has happened. Where is Rosalinde?' His anxiety was ramping up now, as Rosalinde was nowhere to be seen.

Mathilde took a deep breath, as she wondered how to begin telling JJ what was going on. 'Jean-Jacques, there is no easy way to say this. So much has happened since you went away. I will tell you the full story later, but for now, the most urgent thing is that Rosalinde has been kidnapped.' She paused to let him take this in, and then continued to explain that they did not know where she was.

'What? Why would someone kidnap her? Are you sure she's been kidnapped and not just left, or had an accident?'

'We have had contact with the kidnapper, so we know it is true,' said Didier, gravely.

'Why have they kidnapped her?' JJ's mind was whirling; he needed some answers quickly, as he was already planning to start a search for Rosalinde.

'Well,' said Mathilde, 'it's a long story. After you left, we discovered that Rosalinde is my deceased son's daughter, therefore my granddaughter.'

'What? Wow! How on earth did that happen?'

'I won't go into it all now, as it is a very long story. Just accept that it is true. Rosalinde and I were just getting to know one another, when she disappeared.' Mathilde was struggling to speak, and tears had begun to gather in her eyes again.

Didier looked across at her. His heart was so sad for her that he decided to take up the story and fill JJ in. 'JJ, if I may call you that, maybe I should carry on the story, as it is becoming a bit too much for Madame.'

Mathilde nodded and wiped her face with her handkerchief. She was feeling overwhelmed and very vulnerable.

'Ok. I shall tell you what happened first and then what we are doing to find her, so you can get the full picture. It began when we noticed Rosalinde had not returned from her walk just before dinner. I went to look for her and found her necklace on the ground near the lake. It was broken, the clasp snapped, and I could see there were signs of a struggle – the grass was disturbed.'

'Mon Dieu! Were there any signs of injury, such as blood?'

'No, nothing like that. It was just that the grass was flattened and broken near one of the trees. So, I returned home and told Madame, and then we sat and waited, hoping she would return. Alas, she did not. Then we got a phone call from the kidnapper, saying that he had Rosalinde and he wanted some jewels that are apparently hidden in the château.'

Didier paused to let this sink in and to steady himself. Mathilde was dabbing her eyes, trying to stop the tears that were slowly falling, and JJ could not believe what he was hearing. Didier got up and walked over to the side table next to the sofa where Mathilde was sitting. He picked up the photo of Rosalinde and gave it to JJ. 'This is what the kidnapper has given us to prove she is alive, but we cannot make out where she could be from the picture.'

'Have you told the police?'

'No, but we have spoken to Monsieur Hubert – Madame's friend, who is a retired police Inspector. The kidnapper told us not to contact the police and said he would be watching us. We used Miss Rosalinde's mobile phone to call him, not the house phone, in case he is listening in.'

'Ok, I have many questions. Firstly, these jewels – do you know where they are?'

'No JJ,' said Mathilde. 'I have heard about them, but it is mostly legend.'

'Please tell me what you know. It would help either to find them, or to tell the kidnapper that there are no jewels and that he must let Rosaline go.'

'Well, when I first came to the château as a young bride, I was told the story of the jewels. They were lost during the Revolution. The family escaped to England, leaving behind their children's governess, who allegedly ran off with the jewels, because when the family returned sometime later there was no sign of the girl or the jewels.'

'Have you ever attempted to look for them?' asked JJ.

'Yes, of course. In my youth I spent many days searching for them, all to no avail. So, I believe, did my mother-in-law and every generation before us. As you can see, JJ, the château and all its outbuildings are vast – some have never been touched since it was built in the seventeen hundreds. If the jewels are here, which I very much doubt, they could be anywhere. I have never seen any sign of them, only heard rumors, which is why I'm so worried about Rosalinde. We are in an impossible situation.'

As she finished speaking, she slumped back in the chair with exhaustion.

'Ok, we must try to think clearly. The jewels are not going to be easily found, so I think we should concentrate on looking for Rosalinde. Please can I look at the photo?'

Didier went over to the side table and picked up the photograph. He looked at it for a few seconds, trying to work out where it could have been taken, but the background was so dark. He carried it across and gave it to JJ, all the time racking his brains to think where she could be.

JJ looked at the photo, then as he saw Rosalinde's face, a huge sob came from him, as he could not hold back his feelings any longer. 'Oh my God!' he cried. 'What are we going to do? Where do we even begin to look for her? We must call the police and get help.'

'No, JJ. Monsieur Hubert is going to help us. For now, we must sit tight and wait for him. If he thinks we should get the police involved, then that is what we shall do,' said Mathilde.

'But Madame, I cannot just sit here doing nothing, whilst Rosalinde is in danger. There must be something I can do. Have you searched the grounds at all?'

'Yes. I have been down to the lake, which is where I found the necklace, but I – well – we were worried about being seen by the kidnapper so there are acres and acres of grounds and outbuildings that have not been searched,' said Didier.

'But we don't even know if she is on the property. She could be miles away,' added Mathilde.

'Ok. I understand why you have done what you have done, but I think we need to be more proactive now,' said JJ. He didn't want to cause them any trouble, but sitting here doing nothing was ridiculous. He looked over at the bouquet of flowers that he had brought to surprise Rosalinde with and suddenly, he felt overwhelmed. He sat back in the chair silent for a moment, managing to compose himself. 'I am going to look for her – I've made up my mind – but I will be careful, so please do not worry. I would also like to speak to your friend, the retired policeman.'

Mathilde looked up at him and could see that his intentions were good and that he would help them. She felt relieved that he appeared to be taking over, because she was exhausted. 'Very well, JJ. I can see your point of view. Didier and I will help as much as possible, but we must be careful not to be seen.'

'Yes, yes, of course.' JJ was beginning to lose patience. 'Now, where have you already looked?'

Didier told JJ where he had searched and suggested new places to look. Then Mathilde took over, whilst Didier made some sandwiches and coffee. As the estate was so big and there were numerous outbuildings, Mathilde went and fetched the map of the estate, so she could point out to JJ exactly where everything was in detail. They ate the sandwiches and drank the coffee while studying the maps, as JJ felt they must not waste any more time. The estate was around forty acres, with various buildings dotted around it, some empty, some with tenants living in.

'I think it best that we divide the whole estate into four quarters,' said JJ.

Didier had already searched most of the area nearest to the château, so they decided to start at the outside edge and work their way back to the château at the centre. It was agreed that JJ would go to the furthest outbuildings that were empty and search them first; Mathilde would ring Monsieur Hubert and tell him what was happening; and Didier would go to the occupied houses and talk very discreetly to the tenants living there.

JJ set off, armed with a map. He decided to drive, because he could cover a bigger area in less time. As he drove off, he felt very apprehensive and worried sick inside about what was happening to Rosalinde. He hoped that they could find her in time, and that the kidnapper didn't lose patience and do anything terrible to her.

Mathilde had recovered some strength when JJ had returned and she decided that, although she wasn't up to searching outside the property, she could have a look around the château for any clues as to where the jewels could be. So, she set off to look in the cellars, remembering that when her son was a small boy, he loved to play hide and seek down there, where there were many rooms and hidey holes.

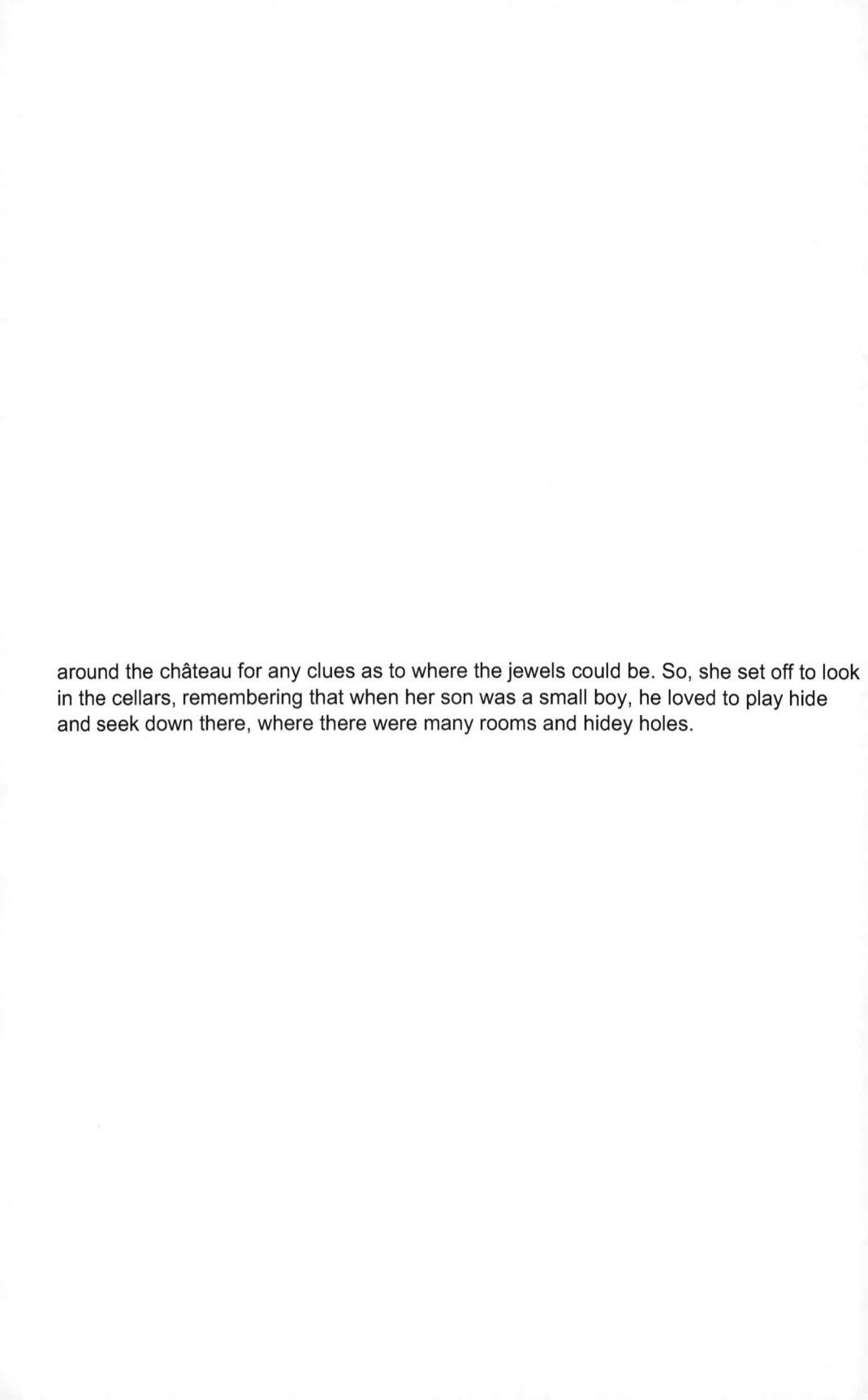

Chapter Sixteen.

Guy was starting to panic. Therese was becoming suspicious, as he had been more agitated than usual, and was in a consistently bad mood these days.

It had started badly this morning when she had asked him why he hadn't gone to work. He had made up some excuse about the old lady being ill and that she wanted peace and quiet, but he knew Therese wasn't buying it. So, he decided he must make an effort to be more like his old self – not over the top, just more civil and relaxed. He wondered how he was going to achieve this, though, with the turmoil that was whirling around in his head.

He wondered what he was going to do with Rosalinde. She wasn't looking too good. If Madame didn't come up with the jewels, how would it all end? He was now beginning to realise he hadn't thought the whole thing through properly. He could be a nasty, miserable git, but he was no murderer. Fortunately, up until now, Rosalinde had not seen his face and he was pretty sure she had not recognised his voice, even though he hadn't disguised it.

He would have to turn up the pressure on Madame La Roche, because time was running out. Rosalinde did not look at all well the last time he had checked on her and the last thing he needed was her dying on him. Guy decided to take Rosalinde some food and then he would ring to find out if Madame had found the jewels. If not, he would give her an ultimatum, because he was convinced they did exist and that she, the high and mighty Madame, was holding out on him. Why wouldn't she give him the jewels when it was her only granddaughter's life at risk? He could not understand why she had not come up with the goods.

Guy got in his car and drove to the large supermarket on the other side of town, all the while racking his brains to think of a way to end the situation that didn't involve violence. He didn't usually shop here, so he hoped no one would recognise him and that he wouldn't bump into anyone he knew. Fortunately, it was almost deserted. He quickly bought some supplies for Rosalinde and then made his way to Château La Roche.

As he neared the château, he noticed a car parked outside one of the old stables. He didn't recognise it and wondered if it was the police. Maybe Madame had broken her word and gone to them for help. 'Oh hell! What am I going to do now?' He decided to hang back, so whoever it was couldn't see him. He would wait for them to come out of the stables, so he could see for himself what was going on and then decide what to do.

Guy didn't have to wait for long; JJ came running out of the stables in a tearing hurry. So that's who it was: the missing boyfriend, of course. He bet Madame and the old butler could not wait to tell him what had happened to Rosalinde.

This put a new perspective on things. Guy was pretty sure he could scare Madame and the old man, but this young buck was not going to be intimidated by him for long. Guy could see from his demeanour that he meant business. If he was going around searching all the outbuildings for Rosalinde, at that pace, it wouldn't take him too long to find her. He was going to have to be very careful; he mustn't be seen under any circumstances.

He did need to get to her and give her some food and water. He deliberated whether to move her, but feared it was too risky. He waited and watched JJ run in and out of the stables. Then when he got into his car and drove off in the opposite direction, Guy got back into his car and drove round to the old building where he was holding Rosalinde prisoner. His mind was turning everything over and over. Should he try and move her? It was a massive risk. He decided to see what sort of state she was in today, but then there was the question of where to move her to. Part of him felt like giving up and letting her go, but he had come so far, and he still hoped the old woman would come up with the goods.

He hid the car around the back of the old barn. There were three grain silos next to the barn, which hadn't been used for a few years, so there was plenty of cover to shield him and the car from plain sight. As he entered the barn, he looked around just before he closed the door, making sure that no one was nearby or watching him. Guy quickly ran up the stairs and pulled the straw bales away from the hidden door. Before he opened the door, he was careful to cover his face. Rosalinde was lying on her side, facing away from him. He crouched down and rolled her over. She looked dreadful. She looked as if she had withered over the last few days; her skin was sallow, and her hair was dull and matted with blood. Guy actually had a pang of regret, because she was a beautiful young woman and he had turned her into this weary, haggard-looking creature.

JJ was frantic. He realised searching all the property on the estate was a fool's errand and Rosalinde might not even be within the immediate vicinity. He had searched several of the outbuildings, to no avail. He sat in his car and got out the map that Didier had given him: there were dozens of buildings, some occupied by tenants, some empty. He could hardly knock on some of the tenants' doors and demand to search their properties. For all he knew, it could be one of them that was holding Rosalinde hostage. No, it was no good. He was going to go back to the château and tell Madame – not ask her; tell her – that they were calling in the police. Rosalinde had been missing for too long now and the chances of seeing her alive were fading. JJ turned the car around and started driving back to the château. It was a beautiful afternoon, and the sun was glinting off the silver grain silos that stood on the edge of the farmyard. It was so bright he had to squint to see where he was going. At the château, Mathilde was standing on the steps looking out for him, wringing her hands with worry.

As soon as he got out of the car, she shouted to him, 'Any sign of her?' Of course, she knew the answer; she could tell by his demeanour.

He walked up the steps wearily and put his arm around Mathilde. 'I'm so sorry, Mathilde. There is no sign of her in any of the places I have looked.' He hugged Mathilde and they both started to cry. 'The time has come to ask for help. I cannot search for Rosalinde by myself. It is too big a task and time is running out. She has been gone too long – anything could have happened to her by now.'

'Yes, you are right. I cannot find any trace of the jewels and I have no hope of finding them. I will phone the police straight away, but we must ensure they are discreet.' She turned and walked into the cool darkness of the château, feeling very downhearted and extremely concerned about what was going to happen next.

Rosalinde had heard the kidnapper arriving and was ready to put on a show of being weak and feeble, although, to be honest, she really didn't need to try too hard. It was daylight, so she could see the outlay of the barn when he released her from the cubby hole. She used the bucket to relieve herself and, fortunately, he turned away as she did so. This meant she could have a good look round and try to orientate herself. She was starving and quickly ate the food he had given her, all the time assessing the place where she was being held. She tried to start a conversation with him, but he was having none of it. He was feeding her and attending to her needs, so he obviously thought she was worth something. This gave her some comfort and she hoped it meant he wasn't going to harm her in any way.

She had noticed there was a bolt on the outside of the cubby hole. If she could find something to undo the bolt when he locked her back in, maybe she could escape. Her eyes fell to the floor, searching for something – anything – that would help her. In the dull, dusty light she could see a rusty nail on the floor near the bucket. If only she could get that, it would help – she was sure of it. The kidnapper got up to put her back in the cubby hole. She would have to act now, or the chance would be lost.

'Please, I need to use the bucket again,' she said in a feeble, pleading voice.

'Ok, but be quick. I haven't got all day.'

Rosalinde sat on the bucket and willed herself to pee. Once again, he had turned his back on her. She decided to cause a distraction by kicking the bucket over, so he would have to deal with it, and she would be able to grab the nail. She just had to make sure the bucket rolled away from the nail, so his attention would be diverted. It was now or never. She got up quietly and pulled up her jeans. Since he was still looking the other way, she thought it prudent to start reaching for the nail before knocking the bucket over. She was halfway to the nail when the bucket went. Guy turned around and saw the bucket rolling on its side, spilling its contents all over the floor.

'You stupid woman!' he shouted, and reached out to pick up the bucket. 'Bloody hell! What a mess you have made.'

Rosalinde didn't care; she had grabbed the nail and hidden it in her sleeve. She thought she had better play along with him, so she acted all sorry. 'I'm sorry. I felt faint and I stumbled,' she lied

Guy looked her up and down; he couldn't tell if she was lying or being truthful. He grabbed her arm roughly and began to tie her hands together. He was furious. He would have to clean up the mess, in case the meddling boyfriend searched the barn. Guy finished tying Rosalinde up and shoved her back into the cubby hole, bolting the door and then replacing the bales of straw. He then turned his attention to the wet patch on the floor. Most of it had seeped into the dry, dusty floorboards so he grabbed a handful of straw and rubbed it into the floor with his foot. He felt confident that it looked ok and if anyone searched the place, nothing would look amiss.

Rosalinde waited until she heard him leave the barn, and then she began to work on freeing herself. She realised if she managed to get her arms and legs free, it was still pretty unlikely she would be able to escape from the cubby hole. She would think about that when she got there. Rosalinde wiggled and jiggled, until she managed to free the nail from her sleeve into the palm of her hand. This had taken some time and considerable effort, so she stopped to rest for a few minutes. It was really difficult to get the nail into the correct position to start rubbing at the rope; her hands kept getting cramp, and her wrists were held so tightly by the rope that it rubbed and chafed as she tried to saw away at it. On and on she tried, stopping every now and then to feel if there was any progress. Because it was so dark in the cubby hole, she could only tell by feel how it was going.

After what seemed like hours, she decided to change tack and try picking at the rope instead. She could feel a tiny bit of fraying rope that had come loose. This encouraged her to try harder. 'Yes,' she thought. 'I can definitely feel it loosening.' Holding the nail carefully in one hand, she tried pulling her wrists apart. The rope began to give; it was loosening. She tugged and tugged with every bit of strength she had and eventually her left hand slipped free. The elation she felt was overwhelming and she burst into tears. Taking a deep breath, she pulled herself together and unwound the rope from her right hand. She rubbed her wrists where the rope had dug in and left its mark. The feeling was coming back into her hands and wrists and she sighed with relief. Although she was exhausted, her success buoyed her, and she quickly set about freeing her feet, which were tied at the ankles. She could sit up in the space, so it was easy to reach her feet and she quickly managed to undo the knot and free her legs. Now, I have to find a way out of here. She got onto her knees and used her hands to feel all along the walls to see if there was any way out.

She searched every inch of the walls, feeling in every gap and in and around every stone. The walls were solid. Of course they were, she thought. This building has been here for hundreds of years. She sat back down, exhausted; even a small amount of activity tired her. When she felt strong again, she decided the roof was next. She ran her hands across the beams; she could feel the slates held in place by old, rusty nails, but there was nothing to help her escape. Every now and then, she came into contact with old dusty cobwebs and all manner of detritus. If only she could see – it was so dark. Her eyes had accustomed to the lack of light, but it was impossible to make out any details. She slumped back down onto the floor; the roof was solid. It was almost too much for her and she felt tears beginning to well up in her eyes.

She pulled herself together. The floor was her last option. Rosalinde got up onto her knees and made her way to the far right corner. She bent forward and started to feel her way across to the opposite corner. She ran her fingers over the ancient, wooden boards that made up the floor. They ran vertically up and down the length of the cupboard – old and dusty – and she wondered how long they had been there. She had been two thirds of the way across when she suddenly realised the boards had changed direction. She felt very excited. She ran her fingers around the boards where the direction changed and felt a two-foot square area. It had to be a trapdoor; what else could it be?

Her excitement was growing rapidly. She felt all around the area again, all the time telling herself to keep calm. Somewhere, there must be a way of opening it. She felt all across it and then felt a tiny hole halfway along one side. She could just poke her finger into the hole, but it was so full of muck and dust she couldn't get it in far enough to pull the trapdoor open. Then she remembered the nail: she could use it to gouge out the hole and maybe even lift the door.

Rosalinde flattened her hands onto the floor and swept them across the boards to find the nail that she had dropped in her excitement at getting free. Her fingers soon found it in the dark, and she quickly put it into the hole and started to clean out hundreds of years' worth of muck. It wasn't long before she had cleared the hole and this time when she tried, she could get her finger all the way in. With her finger in the hole, she could tell the wood of the trapdoor was not too thick, so she tried to pull it up. It wouldn't budge, she sat back disappointed, but she was not going to give up. If she ran the nail around the edge of the trapdoor, it might help to loosen it, she thought. She found the edge with her nails, pushed the old nail in and scraped away. Lots of dust and grime flew out, which gave her renewed hope.

Right, she was ready to try again. This time, she put her finger into the hole and hooked it underneath. She took a deep breath and pulled as hard as she could. It moved; she couldn't believe it. Again, she took a deep breath and pulled. This time it came up about half an inch, just enough for her to get all her fingers under it and pull with all her might. With a lot of creaking and groaning, finally it came free and she found herself looking down into darkness.

Chapter Seventeen.

'They are here,' said Didier, who had been looking out of the salon window. He could see the police car coming slowly up the driveway.

JJ had returned from his search and insisted that Mathilde called them. He had said enough was enough; they could no longer waste time trying to find Rosalinde on their own.

'Let them in, Didier,' said a weary Mathilde. She knew she was going to have to tell the police everything and was not looking forward to reliving it all again.

Didier showed them into the salon, where they introduced themselves. In charge was Inspector Gérard. He had been with the force for seventeen years and was a very experienced officer, but he had never had to deal with kidnapping before. His deputy was Lieutenant Le Brun, a weaselly little man with tobacco stained fingers and a ridiculously droopy moustache.

Mathilde sent Didier to make some coffee and then the detectives sat down. She began to tell them exactly what had happened – about the telephone calls from the kidnapper, about Didier and JJ searching for Rosalinde – and she showed them the photo that the kidnapper had sent to them.

Every now and then she would dab at her eyes. She was losing hope that she would ever see her granddaughter again. They listened patiently until Mathilde had finished and then Inspector Gerard sat forward in his chair. He had remained quiet the whole time Mathilde was speaking. Now it was his turn to speak. 'Madame La Roche, may I ask if you and your granddaughter are close?'

'Well, Inspector...' Mathilde took a deep breath and cleared her throat. 'The truth is I had never met her until ten days ago. She is my son's daughter, born after his death. She has grown up in England with her mother.'

'So, can I assume from that you are not particularly close?'

'Look, I'm sorry,' interrupted JJ, 'but how is this going to help find Rosalinde?'

A very frosty Inspector Gerard looked across the room at JJ and asked very abruptly, 'Who are you?'

JJ was slightly startled at Gerard's tone and it shook him up a bit. 'I am – that is I was – Rosalinde's work colleague, but now we have become closer than that.' He was worried about what to say, because he wasn't sure how much Mathilde knew about his and Rosalinde's relationship.

'It's alright, JJ. I would have to have been blind to not see what was going on with the two of you,' said Mathilde.

'So, the two of you were in a relationship. How long has this been going on?'

'I only met Rosalinde a few weeks ago, too, when we started working together. But I can tell you, our feelings for one another are real and I am desperate to find her.'

'So, you have only met Rosalinde recently, like Madame La Roche?'

'Yes, that is true, but it makes no difference to how I feel about her.'

Gerard paused for a moment, rubbing his bottom lip with his index finger. 'Something doesn't add up here,' he said. 'Le Brun, please can I talk to you in private for a moment?"

Gerard and Le Brun went out into the hallway, leaving Mathilde, JJ, and Didier all staring at each other helplessly.

When they returned a few minutes later, both looking extremely serious, Gerard crossed the room to stand directly in front of JJ. 'Monsieur Jean-Jaques Boden, I am arresting you on a charge of kidnap and conspiracy to rob Madame La Roche.'

Before he had finished speaking, Mathilde had let out an audible gasp and burst into tears. Didier stood up to protest, but Gerard was having none of it.

JJ just shook his head and said, 'Inspector, you have got it all wrong. It has nothing to do with me. Please, please – you must look for Rosalinde!'

Inspector Gerard and Lieutenant Le Brun handcuffed JJ and led him out of the room, to take him away to the station. The whole time JJ was protesting his innocence and begging them to search for Ros.

With him safely in the car, Gerard returned to the salon to speak to Mathilde and Didier. 'Madame La Roche,' he began. 'I feel very strongly that JJ is responsible for your granddaughter's disappearance, so we are taking him to the station to question him. I will be sending some officers out to search the grounds and surrounding area. Please do not worry – we will find her.'

'Inspector Gerard, I cannot believe JJ has anything to do with this! He is a lovely young man.'

'I am sorry, Madame, but at the moment it seems very likely to me that he is responsible. Of course, I will listen to his side of the story, and then I will make up my mind whether to proceed with the arrest or let him go.'

Mathilde was horrified; surely JJ was not involved! She could see how much he loved Rosalinde.

'Madame, I'm sorry to say that in most of these types of crime the victim is known to the perpetrator.' And with that parting statement, he left.

Mathilde and Didier sat quietly, each staring into space, trying to comprehend what had just happened.

Eventually, Didier broke the silence. 'Madame, I just don't believe it. That Gerard is an idiot! I've been sitting here thinking about this. It has all happened very suddenly. We have had very few visitors for years and then, all of a sudden, we had the two bumbling old men looking for work, who I had to dismiss. Now we have this man claiming to be an electrician, who keeps poking his nose in everywhere. What do you think about him?'

'What do you mean Didier?' asked Mathilde.

'Well, I was just thinking, he was here all the time that Miss Rosalinde was here, and I kept finding him poking his nose into places he had no business being in. To add to all that, I haven't seen him for days.'

'Do we have a letter or something from the company he works for?'

'I don't think so, Madame. I will go and check, but I think there is something odd about him.'

'Very well, Didier. Do it quickly. We must find out what is going on and try to help JJ, as well as Rosalinde.'

Didier hurried off to his office, where he kept all the household accounts, to look for any sort of paperwork to do with the mysterious electrical workman.

Mathilde gazed out of the salon's long, elegant windows, across the lawn to the grand, old chestnut tree standing on the edge of the drive. It was at its most beautiful this time of year, but somehow its beauty was lost on her today. All she could think about was the awful mess they were in: Rosalinde missing and JJ carted off by the police, like a common criminal. She felt completely helpless. She was an old woman; how on earth was she going to be of any use in the search for her granddaughter? Mathilde hoped Didier could come up with something to at least help free JJ from the clutches of the police, who – she had already decided – were incompetent.

Didier came sweeping back into the salon in a great rush. 'Madame, I could not find any records or paperwork regarding the electrician,' he said.

'Well, Didier, what does that mean? There must be a letter from the electric company, if he was sent here by them.'

'That is what I thought, Madame, but there is not, so I took the liberty of telephoning the company.'

'And? What did they say?'

'Well, Madame...' Didier paused and took a deep breath. 'They said they had never sent anyone to work on the château and that they had no record of Monsieur Bernier, which I expect is a false name anyway.'

Mathilde stood quietly for a moment and then suddenly flew into a ball of energy. 'You know what this means, Didier?'

'Yes, Madame. He is an imposter. It also means he could be the kidnapper.'

'I will ring the Inspector immediately and tell him what we have discovered.'

Guy had returned to his home but was feeling uneasy. Luckily, Therese, his girlfriend, was at work, so he threw himself down on the sofa and cradled his head in his hands. What had he done? He had been an absolute fool! How did he think he would ever get away with this? He was swiftly concluding that he was going to have to let Rosalinde go; he didn't want a dead body on his hands. She had looked so weak this morning, he feared next time he went to the barn she might be dead. It was lunchtime, but he couldn't eat; he was so torn up inside. He lay down on the sofa and cried himself to sleep.

When he awoke a couple of hours later, he had decided what he was going to do. Guy was pretty sure Rosalinde hadn't seen his face, so he felt confident that if he let her go, she would not be able to identify him. He looked at his watch and it was just gone five o'clock. He would go to the barn now and free her – leave her somewhere, where she would be found quickly and get some medical help. He moved earnestly now. He felt he was doing the right thing; he also wanted to get out of the house before Therese got back from work and started asking awkward questions.

He drove to the barn, panicking, hoping Rosalinde was still alive. Before he had left home, he had put bin bags and a shovel in the boot, just in case, but really didn't want to contemplate what that meant. He hoped the coast would be clear and that he could get her out of the barn without too much trouble. Maybe if he left her near the lake, someone would find her fairly quickly, or maybe he should phone the château and tell them where he was leaving her. He was so confused. It had seemed like such a good idea in the beginning, but now it was all falling to pieces in front of him. He never meant for anyone to get badly hurt; he really thought the old lady would pay up without too much fuss. Now he was really scared. If they found out it was him, well, prison was something he didn't want to think about. His life would be over! Therese would leave him for sure, and he would never have the life he had wished for.

He arrived at the barn, cautiously looking around to make sure the coast was clear. Outside the barn, everything looked normal. Guy drove his van round to the back of the barn, into the dark shade behind a group of fir trees. He turned the engine off and sat still, listening. He could hear the birds singing in the trees and see the blue hydrangea bushes swaying in the slight breeze. Guy carefully opened the van door, trying not to make any noise, and crept around the side of the barn to the front door. He quickly entered the barn and then let his eyes adjust to the darker interior. He paused, listening, in case anyone was waiting to catch him. It was silent, apart from the birds singing.

Guy crossed to the stairs and began to remove the bales of straw covering the door to the cupboard, where Rosalinde was being held. Quickly, he dragged the bales away and slid back the bolt on the old, wooden door. It was so dark in the cupboard that it took a moment for his eyes to adjust again. When he could see clearly, he leaned in to pull Rosalinde out. She wasn't there! What? Where could she be?

He got right inside the cupboard and felt all around in the darkness: no sign of her. She had disappeared! 'This can't be happening,' he thought. He shook his head, as if it would make him see more clearly, but no, she had disappeared.

He ran. Was this a trick? Were they waiting for him outside?

He wasn't going to hang around to find out. Guy fled down the stairs and out to his van, expecting someone to jump out at any moment and arrest him, but no one appeared. He got into the van and drove away as quickly as possible, his heart pounding. How on earth had she got out? Someone must've found her and rescued her. Everything was going round and round in his brain. What the hell was he going to do now? He was so full of adrenaline that he couldn't go home to Therese; she would know something was wrong straight away. He drove into Pontorson and parked down by the river. He sat, staring into the river like a zombie. He couldn't figure out if Rosalinde had escaped, or if someone had found her and set her free. He realised it would only be a matter of time before someone connected the kidnapping to him. The question was, should he stay and act innocent, or run and try to get away before they came looking for him?

Chapter Eighteen.

As the evening began to darken, Rosalinde had no idea what was happening in the outside world. After she had climbed down through the trapdoor, she found herself in a stone tunnel in complete darkness. She began to feel her way along the rough stone walls, bending and stretching to feel the width and height of the tunnel. Rosalinde had no idea where she was or where the tunnel would lead to, but that was not going to stop her. She had to find a way out before the kidnapper discovered she was missing, because she was sure he would come looking for her.

The floor of the tunnel was quite smooth, even though it was bare earth, and the walls felt like a properly built stone, not hacked out bedrock, so she thought she was probably above ground, for now anyway. Rosalinde had only travelled about one hundred yards before she had to sit down. She was exhausted. Apart from the days of very little food and drink, she had been hit on the head and it was all taking its toll. Her head felt sore and at times she felt a little dizzy.

As soon as she got her breath back, she was off again. She detected a slope in the floor of the tunnel and the walls started to narrow slightly. The walls were very damp, and she could hear water trickling down the wall on one side of her. If only she could see, but it was so dark she couldn't even see her own hand in front of her. She kept on feeling her way. As the tunnel went further down, it also got colder and damper; this slowed her even more. Once more she stopped. She sat down, wrapping her arms around her and rubbing them up and down, trying to get warm. The tunnel felt as if it went on forever! In reality, she had only travelled about three hundred yards, but she had no concept of the length of it or the time she was taking. She got up again, determined to carry on and find a way out.

She hadn't gone much further when she felt the tunnel start to widen. First, she felt the left wall and then the right. Yes, it was wider here, she thought. She was walking with her hands out in front of her, palms up and flat, when she bumped into what felt like a wall in front of her. 'Oh no! Please don't let it be a dead end,' she prayed. She began to feel all along the wall, top to bottom and left to right. Straight away, she realised the tunnel forked into two. There were two tunnels in front of her now: left and right.

Oh God! What to do now? How would she choose? There was no point deliberating; she would just have to go down one of the tunnels, hoping it was the right one, and if not, travel back to this point and then try the other tunnel. She chose the left-hand tunnel, as it made no difference; the quicker she moved, the quicker she would hopefully be out of there.

As she travelled down the damp, dark tunnel, she wondered where on earth she could be. Where did this tunnel lead, if anywhere at all? She had no concept of time, or how far below ground she was. Once again, exhaustion overwhelmed her, and she sat down and lent against the wall of the tunnel. In no time, she had fallen asleep; even the desperation to get out of the tunnel could not keep her going.

'Madame, I have just spoken to Inspector Gerard, and I have given him the information about the electrician,' said Didier.

'Good. Now, maybe, they will see sense and release JJ,' replied Mathilde.

'Let's hope so.' Didier was exhausted. He was not a young man and these last few days had taken their toll on him.

'Madame, would you like some dinner?' Didier was very concerned for Mathilde's health, as she had hardly eaten anything for the last few days.

'No, Didier, I cannot eat. My stomach is in turmoil, what with Rosalinde missing and now JJ being arrested.'

'Madame, you really must eat something. Otherwise, you will become ill, and then you will be of no help to Miss Rosalinde when she returns.' Didier decided to use some psychological persuasion to get her to eat.

'Oh, very well, but not a full meal – just something very light. Some eggs, perhaps.'

'Very good, Madame. I will go and make you an omelette straight away.' Off he went to the kitchen, before she could change her mind.

Meanwhile, Gerard was considering what Didier had told him. After questioning JJ and checking his alibi, he was beginning to realise he was barking up the wrong tree.

He needed to find out who this person was that had been working at the château. It was all very suspicious, and Gerard was now convinced this was the man they were looking for. The trouble was they had nothing to go on. He was obviously an imposter. The electric company had confirmed that they had not sent anyone to work at the château and, indeed, that they had never heard of Alain Bernier, which was bound to be a false name in any case.

He needed to find some hard evidence and fast; a young woman's life was at stake here.

Guy had returned home. Therese was already home and had started dinner. As he walked into the flat, she turned to look at him. He looked dreadful; he no longer had the energy to hide his shame and fear over what he had done.

'Where have you been?' asked Therese. She was puzzled at his demeanour.

Guy paused for a moment. He was almost about to confess to Therese, but at the last minute he chickened out. 'Oh, just out – to the château.'

'What has happened? Don't lie to me – I can tell something is wrong.'

Again, he nearly cracked and told her the truth, but he was a coward. 'The van broke down,' he lied.

'Oh, is that all? I thought someone had died, the way you looked.'

At this, Guy left the room. He went into the bathroom and turned on the shower. He was shaking from head to toe. He knew he must control himself. Therese was no idiot; he would only be able to keep her from the truth for so long. He stood under the shower, tears pouring down his cheeks, trying to think of a way out of this mess. Realising he had been in the shower much longer than normal, he pulled himself together and climbed out.

Therese knocked on the door. 'Dinner is ready,' she said quite sharply. 'Are you going to be very long?'

He took a deep breath and replied as calmly as he could, 'No, I am just coming.'

He was going to have to put on the performance of a lifetime this evening!

Inspector Gerard wasn't ready to let JJ go. Even though he was now sure he was not involved with Rosalinde's kidnap, he thought if he let him go, he would hamper the investigation and get in the way. Gerard was a man who liked to be in charge, and he wanted to run the show his way.

Gerard had sent a team of officers out on a search party. They started at the lake, where Didier found the necklace, and fanned out in a circle from there. He had fifty officers out searching, but it was like looking for a needle in a haystack. By nightfall, they had come up with nothing, not so much as a trace. He decided to stand them down until daylight. Fortunately, at this time of year it was light very early, so the search would not be called off for long – just enough time for food and a few hours of sleep, then the search could begin again in earnest.

The next morning, Gerard decided to send the search teams to all the outbuildings. Even though Didier and JJ had been around most of them, they didn't have the training that his officers did. They might find something that Didier and JJ had missed. When they had the planning meeting first thing in the morning, Gerard could not believe how many buildings there were and the size of the estate. He was also mindful that Rosalinde could have been taken away from the château grounds. If only they could find something, but at present they had nothing at all.

With fifty officers combing the grounds, Gerard had set up a command centre on the courtyard at the front of the château. He had maps of the château and the surrounding area set out on tables, under a fairly substantial gazebo. The officers manning the radio were in one corner; a coffee machine stood in another corner; and a group of officers grouped around a table watching a monitor. On the monitor was live footage from a helicopter that was hovering over the estate. Gerard was throwing everything at this case; he was determined to find Rosalinde and was going to leave no stone unturned. To be truthful, he had not had a lot of success lately in his career and he needed this case to have a good outcome. His bosses had been keeping a close watch on him recently; he had been warned to pull his socks up or risk losing his job.

Didier had told the Inspector about the electrician and had said he would have no trouble identifying him. Gerard had brought with him this morning a police artist – Quentin – and he and Didier were busily working on a likeness of the electrician in the château.

Gerard sat pouring over the maps. If only they could find something! Although he wasn't entirely convinced that Rosalinde was being held on the estate, something deep down inside told him she was nearby. Time was running out and there had been no contact with the kidnapper in the last twenty-four hours. If he was suspicious, he may well do something drastic. Gerard knew if Rosalinde wasn't found alive and well, he would be blamed. He sat with his head in his hands, praying that they would find her.

He heard a car coming up the drive; it was being driven very fast. Gerard looked up to see it was Lieutenant Le Brun. The car screeched to a halt in front of the gazebo and Le Brun leaped out of it and ran into Gerard. He was waving an evidence bag. 'Oh, thank God!' thought Gerard. 'At last – a breakthrough.'

'Inspector!' shouted the officer. 'We have something.'

'What is it?' Gerard said, leaping to his feet.

'It's a credit card receipt,' Le Brun replied. He was breathless with excitement.

Gerard slumped back down into his chair. 'Is that all? It could have been dropped by anyone.' Gerard was not impressed.

'But, sir, it is something. We have also found some tyre tracks next to where we found the receipt.'

'Ok, that sounds more promising. What is the receipt for?'

'Diesel, sir.'

'Right, let's get a trace on it and find out whose receipt it is. Then we will pay them a visit and ask them what they were doing on the estate.'

'Right away sir,' said Le Brun.

Maybe this was the turning point they needed, thought Gerard. Le Brun was in the corner of the gazebo on his mobile phone, giving the details on the receipt to an officer back in the main office. He then hung up and came over to where Gerard was sitting. The men's demeanours had completely changed in the last few minutes; they were both much more alert and ready to spring into action, as soon as the information came through from headquarters.

Rosalinde had slept fitfully for several hours in the tunnel. When she awoke, she was so cold and stiff she could hardly move, but she knew she must. The tunnel was freezing cold and the dark walls had water running down them, making everywhere damp. She was worried the kidnapper must have discovered she was missing by now and was probably searching for her. She must get going. Pulling herself up onto her feet, she wrapped her arms around her chest and rubbed her shoulders, trying to bring some warmth back into them. Rosalinde was very weak, but the thought that she was free was spurring her along. The tunnel was narrow and winding. It also began dipping down, going further underground. She came to another fork in the tunnel. This time it reduced her to tears. Was she never to escape this torture? Exhaustion overcame her again; she sat down to rest and before long had fallen asleep.

'Yes, yes, I've got that. Ok, thank you,' said Le Brun. He turned to Gerard, who had been alerted by the phone ringing and was keen to hear what Le Brun had just been told.

'Well?'

'We have a name and address: Guy Moreau of Avenue de Mortain, Avranches. And he is known to us, for petty theft and unpaid speeding fines,' gushed Le Brun.

'Right,' said Gerard. 'Let's go.'

They got up and ran to the car, eager to get to Guy as quickly as possible. Le Brun shouted out that another team would meet them at the address. They were taking no chances; if this was the kidnapper, he was not going to get away.

Avranches was about twenty minutes away from the château. Gerard wanted to approach Guy Moreau quietly, so as not to alert him and scare him off, so there were no sirens or flashing lights. They arrived in Avranches and turned into the narrow street, which housed Moreau's flat. It was not a tall block – only three floors – and the other team of officers had already taken up position. Gerard climbed out of the car and looked up at the flats: pretty run down and shabby, he thought. God! He hoped this was their man and that he was not going to be too much trouble. At sixty-two, he was getting too old for this; chasing criminals was a young man's game.

Gerard approached the front door to Guy Moreau's flat quietly. When everyone was ready, he knocked.

Therese answered, her eyes widening when she saw there were police officers at the door.

'Bonjour, Madame. Is Monsieur Moreau at home?' enquired Gerard.

In the background, Gerard could hear a chair being scraped back across the floor. He wasn't going to wait for an answer. He pushed passed Therese, just in time to see Guy trying to escape onto the balcony. Unfortunately for Guy, Gerard had contemplated this, and his officers were lying in wait. After a brief scuffle, Guy Moreau was led away in handcuffs, to the astonishment of his girlfriend, Therese. Gerard decided not to bother giving Therese an explanation; there would be time for that later. Whilst trained officers searched the flat, Gerard accompanied Guy to headquarters to question him.

Guy was sitting in an interview room, with one policeman guarding the door and another outside the door. There was no point in trying to escape. He sat there, waiting to be grilled by the Inspector. He was white and shaking. He knew they had got him, but he couldn't work out how. He had been photographed and fingerprinted when they bought him in, so he knew this was not over non-payment of speeding fines.

When the Inspector finally appeared an hour and a half later, Guy shrunk down into his chair, trying to curl up into a ball and shut everything that was happening out.

Gerard swept into the room full of confidence, a folder in his hand, which he slapped down onto the table in front of him. 'Bonjour, Monsieur Moreau. I am Inspector Gerard. My colleague, who will be joining us at any minute, is Lieutenant Le Brun.'

As soon as the words were out of Gerard's mouth, Le Brun came rushing into the room, also carrying a folder.

'Do you know why you have been arrested?' Gerard asked.

Guy lifted his head, looked Gerard in the eye, and spoke very quietly. 'Non, Monsieur.'

'Come on, Moreau. Let's not play games. You and I both know that you are responsible for the kidnap of Miss Rosalinde Wilson.'

'I do not know anyone of that name.'

'You dropped a receipt for diesel fuel on the property of Madame La Roche, Miss Wilson's grandmother.'

'So? How does that make me guilty of kidnap?'

'What were you doing on the property?'

Guy thought, if this was the only evidence they had against him, it was very weak. Suddenly he felt more confident and decided to try and talk his way out of it. 'I have been working for Madame La Roche,' he said confidently.

'Is that so? How do you explain the fact that the company you claim to work for has never heard of you?'

The atmosphere in the room changed, as Guy realised they knew more than they were letting on. He decided to keep quiet. 'No comment.'

'Ah,' said Gerard. 'I thought you might say that.'

Le Brun opened his folder and took out the police drawing that the butler had helped to create. He placed it next to the photo that had been taken of Guy on his arrest. 'This is an artist's impression made by a witness, and it bears an uncanny resemblance to you,' said Le Brun.

'No comment,' said Guy. He was beginning to shake again. He kept thinking of the empty hiding place. Had they found her? Was she still alive? How on earth was he going to get out of this?

'May I remind you that if found guilty of kidnap, you face years in jail, but murder is a whole different ball game: murder means life behind bars.'

At this, Guy cracked. He started to sob, quietly at first, then louder, rocking backward and forwards in his chair, mumbling to himself, and holding his head in his hands. Gerard and Le Brun sat back and watched him. They knew he was on the edge and would confess at any moment; they had seen it all before.

'Ok,' said Guy. He was starting to calm down. Maybe Rosalinde was still alive. He knew he was trapped. 'I confess. I kidnapped her.'

'Right, ok. Where is she?' asked Gerard.

Guy sighed. He didn't know what to say. Would they believe him anyway? 'The truth is I don't know.'

'So, you are confessing to kidnap, but you don't know where your victim is? Is that correct?'

'Yes, that is correct.'

Chapter Nineteen.

Gerard could no longer hold JJ legitimately, so, after warning him to stay out of the police's way, they released him. While JJ had no intention of listening to Gerard, he decided he would tread carefully and be discreet in his search for Rosalinde.

JJ made his way to the château and went straight into to see Mathilde. She was very pleased to see him, as was Didier. They assured him that they had never believed the kidnapping was anything to do with him. Mathilde told JJ about Guy Moreau's arrest and that he had confessed to the kidnap of Rosalinde.

'But where is Rosalinde?' he asked.

'That is the problem. Although Moreau has confessed, he has not revealed where he was holding Rosalinde. He has told them that he does not know where she is,' said Mathilde.

'Well, I will begin searching again. I know the police have told me to stay out of it, but I can't – I love Rosalinde.'

At this Mathilde broke down and began to cry. 'I know you do – it is obvious. And she loves you – that is obvious too.'

'Do you know where the police found the receipt belonging to Moreau?' asked JJ.

'We know it was on the property – on the outskirts of the old farm, we think,' said Didier.

'Do you think you could show me on the map?'

'Yes, of course. It's in the study. Would you like to come in there with me?' asked Didier. Didier was desperate to get JJ away from Mathilde, so he could talk to him without her hearing. Luckily JJ picked up on the signals and they both went off into the study. 'Thank you, sir. I wish to speak to you, but I don't want Madame to hear.'

'Of course. I think I know what you are thinking.'

'I am most concerned. The fact that they have not found Miss Rosalinde is very worrying. I'm sure Madame is thinking the same, but I don't want to say it in front of her.'

'Yes, I can see your point.'

'Madame's health is extremely fragile. She is already on the verge of collapse, so we need to speak very cautiously around her.'

'Of course. I understand. Now please let me see this map – I really need to start my search for Ros.'

Didier crossed over to the large, antique desk and pulled the estate map out from under a pile of papers. It was an old map, worn and faded, but as nothing much had changed on the estate for years, it was pretty accurate. The two men pored over the map, Didier pointing out various places. He then indicated the area where the police had found the diesel receipt. JJ scrutinised this area: there were several old barns, but no one occupied the property. It was a quiet and secluded spot, off the beaten track – in fact, a perfect place to hide someone!

'Ok. I will go there now and begin to search. If the police are there, I will keep out of sight,' said JJ.

'But, JJ, it's going to be dark soon. Wouldn't it be better to wait until morning?' As soon as the words left his lips, Didier knew he had said the wrong thing.

JJ turned to face Didier and got right up close to him. In a very small, controlled voice, he said, 'She may not have that long.'

Didier shook his head in despair. 'I am sorry. Of course, you must go and look for her, but have you eaten?'

'No – there is no time for that. Anyway, I can't eat. I must go – I need to find her.'

JJ gathered up his mobile phone and a jacket and ran out to his car. He sped off in the direction of the barns, looking at the night darkening around him. Thank God the police had let him go. He would find her; he had to!

As JJ drove off in one direction, Gerard and Le Brun were driving towards the château. They had come to update Madame La Roche. Unfortunately, there was not much to say, but they felt they should come in person to tell her the latest news.

Didier showed them into the salon, where Madame was sitting. Gerard thought she looked exhausted and he was not looking forward to the conversation they were about to have.

'Bonsoir, Madame.' Gerard and Le Brun both spoke at the same time. They glanced sideways at each other, Gerard giving Le Brun a silent signal to shut up.

'Bonsoir, Inspector. I believe you have some news for me, but, of course, what I really want to know is have you found my granddaughter?'

'Well, Madame, would it be alright if Le Brun and I sat down? As you can imagine, it's been a very long day.'

'Yes, of course, but please get on with what you are going to say. I can't bear people who sugar coat things!'

'Very well. You may have heard that we have arrested Guy Moreau, the man who was working here, allegedly from the electric company.'

'Yes, I know that,' said Mathilde.

'Ok. Well, he has confessed to taking your granddaughter, but he has yet to tell us where he hid her.'

'Do you have any idea of her whereabouts now?' asked Mathilde.

Gerard sighed and looked down at the floor; Le Brun ran his fingers through his hair and looked very sheepish.

Before they could answer, Mathilde spoke again. 'I take it from the look on your faces, the answer is no.'

She was beginning to get upset, which was the last thing Gerard wanted to happen, because what he was going to say next was going to be extremely hard for them all. 'Madame, I'm sorry – we do not know where she is, and he will not tell us anything.' Gerard took a deep breath – he had a very heavy heart – but Mathilde had said she didn't want things sugar coated. 'Madame, your granddaughter has been missing for some considerable time and there is, at the present moment, no sign of her. We must, therefore, accept the fact that she may not be found alive.'

Mathilde had been dreading this moment. She knew it was coming and had tried to push it out of her mind. All of a sudden, it was as if a dam had burst: she started to cry and then she screamed; she couldn't breathe and the pain in her chest, which had been niggling away for days, exploded; she tried to get up, but fell to the floor clutching at her chest.

'Quick! Phone for an ambulance – she's having a heart attack!' cried Didier.

Mathilde writhed on the floor in agony and then, abruptly, she became very still. Didier was bending over her, trying to loosen her blouse, tears falling from his eyes, saying a silent prayer. He could hear Le Brun on the phone asking for an ambulance, but he feared it would be too late.

Gerard swung into action. He knelt down on the floor next to Mathilde and began CPR. He had been trained a few years ago but had never actually had to perform it. He just hoped he could remember what to do! The training was one thing; putting it into practice was another. Adrenaline kicked in and it all came back to him. He settled into a rhythm and worked away steadily. Le Brun had gone to the front door to aid the ambulance when it arrived. Didier had gone to fetch some blankets – Gerard had, effectively, sent him off to get him out of the way. It was a good fifteen minutes before the ambulance arrived. Gerard was tiring, but he kept going.

As soon as they came into the room, the ambulance crew took over and Gerard stepped back.

Gerard, Le Brun and Didier waited outside in the hall, for what seemed like an age. Didier was weeping openly; they had been working on Mathilde for too long. He had all but given up, when the door opened and one of the paramedics came out.

'Monsieur?' he tentatively asked.

'She is alive, but very weak.' He looked at Gerard. 'Inspector, you saved her.'

Didier grabbed Gerard and hugged him. 'Monsieur, I cannot thank you enough,' said a weary and emotional Didier.

'She is not out of the woods yet. We must get her to hospital straight away,' said the paramedic.

'May I come with her?' asked Didier.

'Yes, Monsieur. Are you her next of kin?'

'No, I'm not, but – that is – umm –'

Gerard interjected, 'Under the circumstances, I think it would be best if Didier stayed with Madame La Roche. We are in the middle of an investigation involving Madame's next of kin.' He decided now was not the time to go into details, given the urgency of the situation.

The paramedics prepared to take Mathilde away to hospital and Didier very quickly packed a small bag to take with him for Madame.

As an unconscious Mathilde was being put into the ambulance, Didier asked Gerard, 'What is going to happen now? Will you continue searching for Miss Rosalinde?'

'Yes, of course. We are still searching. Tomorrow we are going to start dredging the lake and looking for disturbed ground where a body may have been buried.'

'Oh God!' thought Didier. That was the last thing he wanted to hear. At least Mathilde would be spared that for a few days. He climbed into the back of the ambulance with Mathilde and they sped off to the hospital.

Gerard and Le Brun went back to the control room at the station to make plans for the morning. If they did not find Rosalinde alive and Mathilde didn't make it, Moreau would have two deaths on his conscience.

JJ had searched the old farmhouse, which had been abandoned during the war. It looked as if no one had been in it for years. It was still full of furniture, all rotting away, festooned with grey, dusty cobwebs. 'Antique dealers would have a field day in there,' he thought. There was no sign of disturbance, so he moved on to the outbuildings. There were several old barns and cow sheds grouped around a courtyard. He was running out of places on the estate to search; these were the last buildings. He knew the police would resume their search in the morning and that they would be swarming all over the place, even searching in the lake and ditches. It was so dark, and he only had a torch to see, but he could not stop; he was convinced Rosalinde was nearby. He entered the last barn, tired and hungry now but still determined. It was a vast structure, half filled with straw and hay. Unusually, it had a rudimentary staircase to one side, which went up to a hayloft. He began by searching the ground floor: nothing looked disturbed or out of place. He looked up above him, shining the torch into the four corners of the barn. Suddenly, he felt overwhelmed. He sat down to rest for a few minutes, but within seconds he was asleep.

When he woke, he looked at his watch and, unbelievably, he'd slept for two hours. JJ jumped to his feet and rubbed his eyes; he felt a bit more refreshed now and had renewed energy. He looked at the staircase and, although he thought it an unlikely hiding place, he knew he must check it out. He swiftly climbed the stairs and immediately knew something was wrong here. He could see, even in the dim light, signs of a disturbance on the floor. He moved some straw bales and found an old, galvanized bucket, loo roll, and some rope. When he shone the torch over the floor, he could see something had been split recently. He bent down to sniff at it: urine. This was the place – he knew it. JJ started moving the bales of straw, tearing at them in his hurry. She must be here somewhere.

Then he saw the little door in the wall. He stopped, his heart beating wildly. This was it.

He knelt down in front of the door and found it was bolted and padlocked. He looked around for something to break the padlock with: nothing! He would have to go out to his car and get a wrench. He flew down the stairs and out to his car. Flinging the boot open, he grabbed a wrench from his tool kit and quickly ran back up the stairs. After hitting the padlock several times, eventually it broke apart. JJ slid back the bolt and opened the door, only to find an empty space.

He fell to his knees, head in hands, and howled, 'No, no, no! This has to be the place!'

He shone the torch around the tiny, cramped space. Then he saw something on the floor. He crawled into the cupboard and reached out: a piece of rope, broken, as if it had been torn away. There was enough rope to tie someone's hands and feet. So, she had been kept there, but where was she now?

JJ shone the torch all around the walls, ceiling and floor of the small space. It was very difficult to see in the dark. He had left the floor till last, eventually shining the torch over the old, wooden floorboards. There was something on the floor he hadn't noticed straight away. He could see a series of lines cut into the boards; they formed a square. Of course – he realised straight away it was a trap door! There was no handle set into the door, so he would have to find something to lever it up. In his pocket he had a key; it was just small enough to fit into the tiny gap between the boards. He levered it up and slid the wrench he had broken the padlock with under the door, to hold it up. He managed to half stand up in the cupboard, so he could lift the trap door and look down into the hole below.

Could Rosalinde have escaped? Was she down in this hole? Well, there was only one way to find out! He leapt down into the hole and shone the torch around: a tunnel. 'She must be down here,' he thought. Holding the torch in front of him, he set off down the tunnel. God! He hoped she was here, and he found her in time. The tunnel was so damp and dark; if she was in a bad way, she wouldn't last long. He carried on down the tunnel. He could feel it dipping down under his feet, as it grew colder. He realised the tunnel was going underground, but he couldn't tell which direction he was travelling in. Ahead of him, he could see a fork in the tunnel. He had no idea which fork to take, so he carried on down the left-hand side of the tunnel. Even though he had rested, he was exhausted. Clearly, the strain of the last few days had taken its toll on him. He had to slow down – the cold in the tunnel had got to him and he was struggling – though the thought that he was near Rosalinde spurred him on and he kept going.

The tunnel was still descending and getting colder. 'It must be several feet underground now,' thought JJ. He wondered if it would lead back to the château. These old places always had escape tunnels and secret hiding places dating back years. He looked ahead and could see another fork in the tunnel. Oh no! Which way to go now?

Then he saw something in the shadows: a body. 'Oh my God!' he cried. 'Rosalinde! Rosalinde!'

Rosalinde was on the ground, unconscious. He couldn't wake her, but she was alive. JJ shone the torch over her face; she didn't open her eyes. He could see blood on her head, and her beautiful, blonde hair was matted and filthy. He felt all over her body for broken bones; as far as he could tell nothing was broken, but she was in a hell of a state.

JJ knew he would have to carry her back along the tunnel, which wouldn't be easy, as the tunnel was barely wide enough for him in places. Nevertheless, he had no choice. She needed help straight away: he had taken her pulse and it was very weak; she was badly dehydrated; and the wound on her head looked infected.

At least she was not heavy to carry. He picked her up and cradled her in his arms, as he made his way back down the tunnel, stopping every so often to rest. He trudged on through the tunnel, shining the torch ahead of him, trying to work out what he would do when he got to the trap door. It would be difficult to climb up on his own, let alone with Rosalinde in tow. He carried on, passing the fork in the tunnel. Then he felt the ground start to rise slightly. 'Thank goodness! We must be nearly back to the barn,' he thought. Still, he kept on walking, carrying Ros, who hadn't stirred at all during the journey.

JJ had to stop for a moment; his arms were aching. Although Ros was not heavy, it was still hard work carrying her all this way. He leaned against the wall to rest, Rosalinde strewn across his body. As he sat there, he considered that it had seemed a much longer journey on the way back to the trap door. JJ shone the torch around the walls of the tunnel: they were dry, not dripping and damp as before. Could he have taken the wrong tunnel? He jumped up, leaving Ros on the floor. He decided to carry on a little way up the tunnel, to see if there was another way out. The tunnel was improving; instead of being hewn out of rock, there were ancient stone walls, properly built. They must be near the château. Maybe this tunnel led to the old cellars under the property, he thought.

JJ ran back to Rosalinde, picked her up carefully, and retraced his steps up the tunnel. He wearily staggered along the tunnel, the ground evening out as he went. They had only gone a couple of hundred yards when the torch started to falter, and then the batteries gave up altogether.

'Oh, come on!' shouted JJ. The frustration was just too much. He stopped, put Rosalinde down on the floor, and shook and banged the torch to try to get it going. It was dead. JJ threw it away in despair.

There was nothing for it; they would have to carry on in the dark. He picked Rosalinde up and put her over one shoulder, so he could use his free hand to feel ahead of him. He was hoping his eyes would adjust to the dark, but it was pitch black – he couldn't see a thing!

They continued along the tunnel, JJ feeling the walls on either side of them. The tunnel roof was higher, so it was easier for him to walk; he no longer had to bend down. The tunnel was definitely becoming more refined – the floor was smoother – and JJ really hoped it would end in the château.

Suddenly, he was aware of a sliver of light up ahead. Yes, he could see very dimly, but there was some light. As they got nearer, he could see some sort of gate at the end of the tunnel. On reaching the gate, JJ gently put Rosalinde down onto the floor. He grabbed hold of the gate and pulled; it was solid and would not move an inch. The gate was wrought iron and about seven feet tall, with an arched top. He looked through the gate and could see a small fanlight window at the top of the wall. This was where the light was coming from. They were in the cellar. He was sure of it. He knew the cellars were vast and nobody ventured to the extremities these days. He could see no one had been in this corner for years; it was dark, full of cobwebs and ancient boxes of goodness knows what.

JJ grabbed hold of the gate and shook it again; it was solid and probably rusted shut after years of neglect. His heart sank. He couldn't turn around and go back. It was too far; it would take too long; and there were too many tunnels to negotiate in the dark. He looked at Rosalinde, still unconscious, and knew time was running out for her. He had to get help now. If he could find something to bang and make some noise, Didier or someone might hear him. Looking through the gate, he could see a piece of wood. It was about five feet long and a couple of inches wide. If he could reach it, he could use it to bang on the fanlight window. Bending down, JJ put his shoulder to the gate and squeezed his arm through. It was so close, but just out of reach. Deflated, he brought his arm back through and sat quietly for a few minutes. He must think of something.

Rosalinde had fought her way into the tunnel – God knows how – and he was not going to let her down now.

His belt! If he took it off and bent the buckle over, it would make a hook. Maybe he could throw it over the wood and draw it nearer to him. He swiftly set to work, fashioning his tool. His arm through the gate once more, he tried to lasso the belt around the piece of wood. He tried several times, but it just was not working. JJ sat and rested for a bit and then decided to have one last try, before giving up.

Right. This time he was determined it was going to work. He summoned up every bit of strength he had and threw the belt. He did it. It hooked around the piece of wood and held fast. JJ shifted position and gradually pulled the piece of wood towards him. As soon as it was in reach, he let go of the belt and grabbed the wood. Pulling the wood towards him and then getting it at the right angle to reach the window was very awkward, but he did it. The wood was heavy and JJ was tired, but he knew he could not give up now; they were so close. He lifted the wood and swung it at the window. It hit home. The window shattered instantly, but he kept hitting it, making as much noise as he possibly could.

Didier was in the kitchen, making a pot of coffee for himself. It was very early, but he hadn't been able to sleep after the previous night's events. He heard the sound of breaking glass. He thought it was coming from below him. 'What on earth is happening now?' he muttered, going to investigate. He went out of the back kitchen door and looked around, following the back wall of the house. He spotted some broken glass near one of the cellar windows – that was new. He bent down to look and could see something repeatedly hitting the window frame from inside: a wooden stick? He couldn't see properly from here; he would have to go down to the cellar and see what on earth was going on. It took him a few minutes to get down to the cellar, but when he got there, he could not believe his eyes.

JJ and Rosalinde. JJ had found her. She was alive.

Chapter Twenty.

Didier could not believe it when he found JJ and Miss Rosalinde in the cellar. They were trapped behind an old, iron gate that he had never seen before. He had no idea there was a tunnel leading to one of the old barns on the property. Otherwise, he would have searched there himself.

After trying in vain to open the gate, he had telephoned for help. The rescue team soon had them free, and Rosalinde was taken off to the hospital. JJ would not leave her side, so he was given a bed in the hospital next to her. Rosalinde was found to be suffering from dehydration and hypothermia. She also had a small head wound, but it was not too serious. A few days' rest and rehydration and she would be fine. Didier didn't want to think about what would have happened if he hadn't found them.

Mathilde was doing well and would be allowed home in a few days, so Didier was trying to get the château back in order. The police had left and cleared away their operations room on the front lawn. They had informed Didier that Guy Moreau had been formally charged with kidnap and blackmail and that, at some point, he would be called as a witness. Didier had telephoned Miss Rosalinde's mother and told her the whole story. Mrs. Wilson was now making her way to France to be reunited with her daughter.

A few days later and Mathilde was home from the hospital and awaiting the arrival of Rosalinde, her mother Ellen, and JJ. She was still weak from the heart attack, but knowing her granddaughter was safe had helped her recovery immensely.

Didier came into the salon with morning coffee. 'Madame, I have just had a telephone call from JJ. They are on their way and should be here in about thirty minutes.'

'Oh, that's wonderful, Didier. Is everything ready for them?'

'Yes, Madame. Violet from the village has been and made up the bedrooms for all of them. I have had some food bought in for lunch and dinner, so everything is under control.'

'Thank you, Didier. I don't know what I would do without you,' said Mathilde sincerely.

Didier left the room to carry on with the preparations, giving Mathilde time to reflect on the events of the last few days. They had been to hell and back! Her emotions had been on a rollercoaster for days; no wonder she'd had a heart attack.

Finally, Mathilde could hear a car coming up the gravel drive. She got up slowly and crossed to the window. She saw JJ leap out of the car and rush round to open Rosalinde's door and then help her out of the car. She still looked very weak and Mathilde could see she was leaning heavily on JJ for support. Then Mathilde saw Rosalinde's mother climb out of the back of the car. She was a striking looking woman, who in her younger days must have been incredibly beautiful. Mathilde could see why her son had fallen in love with her and, for a moment, she was overcome with sadness for what might have been. She sighed and pulled herself together, because this was a joyous occasion.

Didier showed them into the salon, where Mathilde was waiting. All decorum vanished as Rosalinde rushed across the room into Mathilde's arms. They both burst into tears, thinking about their ordeal. They soon began to recover and gain some composure. Then the introductions began; Rosalinde's mother, shy at first, came forward and was warmly welcomed by Mathilde. Didier came in with a pot of coffee, which he set on the table with the cups and saucers that were ready and waiting.

'Please join us, Didier,' said Mathilde. 'You are as much part of this story as the rest of us.'

'Thank you, Madame,' he replied. 'I am so pleased you are back safe and well, Rosalinde, and it is lovely to meet you at last, Ellen.'

Ellen Wilson gazed down into her cup of coffee, looking slightly embarrassed.

Mathilde saw this and was quick to react. 'Please don't worry, Ellen. The past is the past. Let's look to the future. I know I may not have a long time in front of me, but I am determined to make up for all the time we have lost.'

'That is very kind of you, Madame,' Ellen replied.

'Please call me Mathilde. We are family, tied together by Rosalinde.'

Mathilde and Ellen both gazed across to Rosalinde, who, despite her ordeal, was looking so beautiful. They then both looked at each other and smiled. Rosalinde was in love; she was radiant and could hardly take her eyes off JJ.

'Now, do you feel ready to tell your story, Rosalinde?' asked Mathilde.

'Yes, but there isn't much to tell.'

'I'm sure it would do you good to get it off your chest,' said Mathilde.

'Ok. Well, it all started when I decided to go for a walk down to the lake, though it gets a bit hazy after that. The next thing I remember is waking up, tied up in a very small space.'

Mathilde and Ellen both gasped in horror.

'The small hayloft in the old barn,' interrupted JJ.

'Yes, that's right.' She shook slightly, as if reliving it, then gave JJ a small smile. 'The kidnapper came and gave me food and drink in the morning and again at night. I had no idea why he had kidnapped me, and I was very scared. My head hurt and I felt so weak. I almost gave up, but something gave me the strength to keep going.'

She paused to take a breath and she could see her mother was quietly crying. 'I had no idea whether it was morning or night, as it was so dark. Anyway, he came to feed me and let me go to the toilet. We will draw a veil over that – I'm sure you don't wish to know – but whilst that was happening, I spotted a nail on the floor and managed to get hold of it without him seeing. When he put me back in the cupboard, I eventually freed myself and found the trapdoor.'

Again, she paused, reliving it all in her head. 'I dropped down into the tunnel and that is where JJ found me.' She looked across at JJ, who was sitting next to her, holding her hand. 'Thank you,' she said and kissed his hand.

Mathilde gazed at them; they were so in love. Thank goodness everything was going to be ok. 'Of course, I knew the tunnels were there under the château, but I have never fully explored them,' she said. 'When I first came here, it was not the done thing to ask questions and go around exploring. My in-laws were very strict about how a young lady was to conduct herself.'

'Madame, if I might speak?' piped up Didier.

'Of course, dear Didier. I don't know what I would have done without you all these years, and especially the last few days.'

'Well Madame, I believe there is an ancient map in the library, detailing the cellars and to some extent the tunnels. The original tunnels have been there much longer than the château, of course. There was a medieval fortress built here before the château and I believe that some of the tunnels date from that time.'

'I would love to look at that map,' enthused JJ.

'Yes, me too,' said Rosalinde.

Ellen looked across at her daughter and could see how exhausted she was. The poor girl had been through an enormous ordeal. 'I think there will be plenty of time for looking at maps. You need to rest now,' she advised.

'Yes, Mum, you are right – I am feeling very tired. I think I will go up to my room and have a lie down.'

'I think it might be a good idea if we all had a rest,' said Mathilde. 'It's been a tough few days for all of us.'

They all got up and one by one headed upstairs to relax before lunch. JJ went with Rosalinde to her room and helped her into bed. He then settled down on the sofa near the window and watched her fall asleep. He was so happy that he had found her and that their feelings for one another were mutual. He lay on the sofa watching her, until he too fell asleep.

Ellen was in her room. The last few days had been a complete whirlwind for her; she found it impossible to sleep; her mind was going round and round. The horror of her daughter's kidnap had traumatised her and, even though she was now safe, she was struggling to come to terms with it. She also felt so guilty for not telling Rosalinde about her father and his family. The thought that a family could be reunited and then cruelly separated within a matter of days was almost incomprehensible. She would have to sit down with Rosalinde and talk it through with her, for both their sakes. Mathilde had been wonderful – very understanding – and as for JJ, Ellen could see how much in love he and Rosalinde were. She hoped they would have better luck than she had.

It was no good – she could not settle – so she decided to go down to the kitchen and see if she could help Didier with the lunch. As she walked along the hallways of the château, she appreciated how beautiful it was. Rosalinde's father had grown up here and she had never seen it, until now. If things had been different, the château may have been her home. That was in the past; she decided to concentrate on the future and was determined to make herself useful whilst she was here.

Didier was preparing a light lunch of soup, bread, cheese and salad when Ellen entered the kitchen. 'Bonjour, Didier.'

'Bonjour, Madame Wilson. How may I help you?'

'I would like to help you, Didier. You and Madame La Roche have done so much to help Rosalinde over the last week. Please tell me what I can do to help with lunch.'

'Oh, it is fine Madame. I can manage.'

'No, really. And please call me Ellen – Madame is so formal.'

'Of course, Ellen, if that is what you wish.' Didier felt slightly awkward calling her Ellen, but he knew there were going to be great changes around the château in the coming weeks, so he had better get used to it. 'I have laid the table in the dining room. If you could perhaps carry through the bread, cheese and salad? Then all I will have to do is bring in the soup when we are ready.'

'Yes, no problem. Do you want me to fetch everyone?'

'Yes, in about fifteen minutes,' said Didier.

Ellen arranged the food on the table and admired the beautiful room; it was so elegant, like a time warp. The furniture was antique and highly polished, not like today's modern surfaces. There were ancient portraits on the walls and a huge fireplace. The bottom half of the walls was covered in old oak panelling, which would have made the room very dark if it wasn't for the three long windows down one side of the room, where the sunlight was flooding in. Above the table was a magnificent chandelier, which she could see had been converted to electricity. She looked at her watch: it was one thirty, meaning Rosalinde had slept for two hours. She would go and wake her for lunch; as well as rest, she needed to eat to get her strength back.

Rosalinde was awake and hungry, so she and JJ needed no persuasion to get up for lunch. They made their way down to the dining room, where Mathilde was already seated and Didier was ladling the soup into bowls. Ellen was sitting next to Mathilde, and Mathilde had asked Didier to join them. Rosalinde was starving but, because she had eaten so little for several days, knew she had to take it easy. JJ, on the other hand, did not hold back; he hadn't eaten for twenty-four hours and was ravenous.

'This is wonderful, Didier. Did you make the soup yourself?' asked Ellen.

'I would like to say yes, but no – Marie Claire from the village made it, Ellen,' he replied.

Mathilde raised an eyebrow at the use of Ellen's Christian name, but then told herself times were changing, and she must accept it. 'Rosalinde, how are you feeling now?' she enquired.

'I am feeling stronger and so happy to be back here. Grandmother, would you be able to tell us more about the tunnels and the history of the château?' she asked.

Mathilde was completely taken aback; it was the first time Rosalinde had called her Grandmother. She raised her napkin to her face to wipe away a tear. This did not go unnoticed by Ellen, who was sitting opposite Rosalinde. 'Well,' she began, after she had composed herself, 'as you know, I came here as a young bride and had to mind my ways, but over the years I have heard and discovered a few secrets of the château.'

'Please, can you tell us anything about these alleged jewels that the kidnapper was after?' asked Rosalinde.

'Yes, yes, of course. I will tell you what I have heard, but please bear in mind it may not be true.'

Mathilde thought for a moment and then recollected, 'The story begins in the 1870s when Comte and Comtesse La Roche lived here with their three children. It is their portrait that hangs in the blue bedroom. The lady in the blue dress is the Comtesse and she looks so like you, Rosalinde – indeed, she is one of your ancestors. They were very wealthy aristocrats, living a charmed life, until the revolution. Suddenly, they and all their friends were in danger. Châteaux up and down the land were being raised to the ground, and aristocrats imprisoned or killed.'

Mathilde shivered as she spoke. 'They escaped to England with their children, grateful to be alive, as so many didn't make it. They fled in a terrible hurry, leaving possessions behind – even the Comtesse's vast jewellery collection. They meant to send someone back for them later. In their haste, they even left behind the children's governess, Sophie, who was a cousin of the Comtesse.

'One night the mob came to the château, looking for anything they could steal and intending to burn the property to the ground. No one knows what happened. The château was ransacked, but not set alight. It has been said that the angry mob made their way to the cellars, found the Comte's considerable wine collection, got very drunk, and then fell asleep. When they awoke the next morning, feeling dreadful, they all went home with their tails between their legs.'

'But what happened to Sophie?' asked Rosalinde.

'Well, that is the mystery – Sophie and the jewels were never seen again!'

'So, did everyone assume she ran away with the jewels?' JJ butted in this time.

'Yes. All the villagers swore there were no jewels to be found in the château and not so much as an earring has ever surfaced since.'

'Could they still be here in the chateau?' asked Rosalinde.

'Who knows? During World War Two, the château was occupied by Nazis. They heard the story of Sophie and the jewels, and they searched for them, but never found them.'

Mathilde stopped talking and took a sip of her drink. She looked around the table at everyone. They were all quiet, thinking about the story she had just told them.

'I think we should look for them, JJ!' exclaimed Rosalinde.

'I was thinking the same,' he replied.

Chapter Twenty-One.

Two days later and Rosalinde was feeling much better. Mathilde's health was also improving, although it was obvious to all that the heart attack had taken its toll on her.

Rosalinde had spoken to her boss at the magazine, Janet Grey, and told her what had happened. She had immediately given Ros indefinite leave to recover and to spend time with her newfound family. In fact, she had been very concerned and sympathetic, which was very unlike her, thought Ros. Ellen had also taken time off work to help look after Mathilde and they were getting on splendidly.

Guy Moreau was in prison awaiting trial, which would take place in a few months. He had admitted to the kidnap and assault of Rosalinde. His girlfriend Therese was horrified when she found out what he had done and had vowed never to see him again.

Rosalinde and JJ were getting on so well: spending time together, relaxing, and enjoying each other's company. They had been picnicking on the château grounds and exploring the woods and countryside around the château. They were falling deeply in love, and Rosalinde knew she had found her soulmate in him.

One afternoon they were sitting under an old oak tree down by the lake.

'JJ, I've been thinking about the jewels,' said Ros.

'So have I!' echoed JJ, jumping up. 'They must still be here, if they have never been seen since the revolution – it's the only conclusion.'

'Yes, that's what I was thinking. Why don't we try to find them?'

'Ok – as long as your grandmother is happy with that.'

'I don't think she will mind, as long as we don't disturb her too much.'

'Ok then, let's go back to the château and take a look at the old maps.'

They gathered up their belongings and swiftly made their way back to the château, chattering excitedly, full of adventure.

They went straight into the library and got out all the old maps they could find.

Didier came in and saw what they were doing. 'Ah,' he said, 'I wondered how long it would take you.' He left the room laughing.

They spent hours poring over the old maps, trying to identify the tunnels that JJ had found Rosalinde in, but they didn't seem to be able to find them on any of the maps.

Didier and Ellen called them for dinner. They hadn't realised the time, so engrossed as they were with the maps. They decided to tell Mathilde at dinner what they were planning. Rosalinde felt slightly nervous about telling her, but decided it was better to be honest.

'Grandmother, JJ and I have been looking over the old maps. We would like to try and find the jewels, if that is ok with you?'

Mathilde looked at Rosalinde very seriously and then spoke. 'I thought you might want to. I have no problem with you looking for the jewels, but please don't become obsessed with it and forget about your real life. I know things like this can become an obsession – look at what has recently happened.'

'No, of course, we will keep it all in perspective. Grandmother, do you have any idea what we might actually be looking for?'

'From stories passed down through the years, all I know is there were a lot of very valuable stones and gold jewellery. If you look at the portrait of the family, the necklace in the painting is one of the items that has never been found. I believe it is made of diamonds and sapphires.'

'Wow! It would be amazing to find that,' exclaimed Rosalinde.

'Don't get too carried away. There have been many, many people over the years, who have searched for them and not found a single trace,' Mathilde said seriously.

Feeling suitably chastised, Rosalinde thought she had better take on a more sober attitude around Mathilde, so she changed the subject.

After dinner, Mathilde retired to bed; she was still feeling very weak from the heart attack. Ellen also wanted an early night, so Rosalinde and JJ were left alone. It was a beautiful evening, balmy, and the sun was still just visible in the sky. They decided to take their coffee out onto the terrace, to enjoy the warm evening and watch the sun go down. On the terrace, Mathilde had some very old, white iron garden furniture with floral cushions, which was surprisingly comfortable. They snuggled up on the largest sofa to watch the sunset. JJ could hardly take his eyes off Rosalinde – she was so beautiful – and Rosalinde felt so safe in his arms. They just lay there together, so happy and grateful to be back in each other's arms. It wasn't long before they fell asleep. It was inevitable really, after the last few days.

When they woke, the sun had gone and the terrace was in darkness, apart from the odd light shining out onto the terrace from the château's upstairs windows. It was almost as if they had stepped back in time. It felt eerie. They got up and made their way indoors to bed. They were both staying in the blue bedroom. Rosalinde switched on the bedside light and glanced across the room to the portrait of the family. In the half-light the jewels shone out; it was as if they were calling to them, 'We are here. Come and find us.' They looked at each other; both knew at the same moment what the other was thinking. JJ took Rosalinde's hand and led her to the bedroom, staring deeply into her eyes.

They quietly and gently made love, both relishing in each other's bodies and feeling secure in their love.

When Rosalinde woke the next morning, she felt so relaxed and calm. She could hardly believe what she had been through over the last few weeks. JJ had already got up and, as she started to do the same, his head appeared around the bedroom door. He was carrying a tray of coffee and croissants, furnished with a little vase of flowers that he had picked from the garden.

'Good morning, Madame,' he said, as he entered the room.

'Bonjour, Monsieur,' Rosalinde replied. She smiled at him, revelling in her good fortune at finding love with him.

'Mathilde is having a lie-in this morning, so I thought maybe we could be a bit lazy and have breakfast in bed.' He handed her the vase of flowers. 'For you, my love,' he said, kissing her.

'Thank you, my darling. Now, hand me those croissants – I'm starving!' she said, playfully.

They took their time over breakfast, chatting and planning their search for the château's jewels. They had already studied the maps and discovered that the tunnels where JJ had found Rosalinde were not documented. They knew there was a labyrinth of tunnels under the château and decided to begin their search in the tunnels that were not mapped. This made sense to them, thinking that others who had searched had probably stuck to the areas on the maps. After breakfast, they showered, making love again in the shower.

They told Didier where they were going to start and took torches and snacks with them. They would probably be out most of the day and didn't want to have to return for lunch.

'I am so excited!' gushed Rosalinde, as they made their way down the cellar steps.

'Me too,' said JJ, 'but we must do this systematically and not get carried away.'

'Of course. Shall we start at the gate where Didier found us?' asked Rosalinde.

'Yes, that's a good place to start. I don't expect you can remember much about your journey through the tunnels.'

'No, I'm afraid I can't. I was so frightened the kidnapper was coming after me. I was also very weak and confused.'

JJ got a notepad and pen out of the rucksack he was carrying, just as they came to the gate. The gate stood open now. Rosalinde shuddered as she approached it, bad memories flooding back.

JJ noticed her hesitation and put his arm around her. 'It's ok, my love.'

'I know – it's just – I didn't think at one point I was going to make it.'

'But you did, and you are fine.'

'Yes. When I am with you, I feel invincible. Come on, let's go – I want to solve this mystery.'

They went through the gate and into the tunnel, walking all the way to the fork and deciding to take the other route, which neither of them had been down before. The tunnels were so cold and damp; Rosalinde shivered as they walked along, shining the torch in front of them. They could feel the tunnel floor starting to dip down as they walked. JJ wrote down the route in his notebook and recorded every twist and turn. He tried to estimate how far they had walked, but it was very difficult in the dark. The tunnel narrowed every now and then and as it got further down into the earth, the colder and damper it became.

'We should have brought a compass with us, so we could tell which direction we were travelling in; it's very difficult and disorientating in the dark.'

'I think I've got one on my phone,' said Ros, diving into her rucksack and fishing out her mobile. 'Now, let's see. I've never used it before.'

They soon got it working and in the dim light, the compass pointed northwest.

'Hum,' said JJ, 'that means we are heading across the old potager.'

'What's that?' asked Rosalinde.

'It's the old vegetable garden. You know – the walled garden with the fruit trees in,' said JJ.

'I wonder how deep underground we are and where this tunnel leads to?' mused Rosalinde.

'Maybe the tunnel links the château's kitchen with the gardeners' area, so they could bring the food to the house unseen in the old days.'

Rosalinde mulled this over in her mind, imagining the hard-working gardeners bringing baskets full of produce and flowers to the château through this tunnel. Somehow it just didn't make sense. 'What is beyond the potager?' she asked.

'Um...' JJ had to think for a minute and then he said, 'The church, I think.'

'Ah, that would make sense. The priest could travel back and forth unseen.'

They carried on down the tunnel, expecting to eventually come to the church. They hadn't gone much farther, when they came to another fork in the tunnel.

'Oh,' said JJ, 'I wasn't expecting that. I thought the tunnel would be a straight run to the church.'

'Well, what do we do now? Should we turn left, or right?'

JJ looked at the compass; he reckoned the right tunnel would lead them to the church, probably into the crypt underneath the building. So, they decided to take the left tunnel. They could always come back and try the right tunnel, if it turned out to be a dead end.

They had been in the tunnels for several hours now. They decided to stop and have their snacks, and some coffee from the flask they had brought with them.

'Do you think we will actually find anything?' Ros asked JJ.

'I don't know, but it is fascinating wondering where all these tunnels go and how they are all connected,' he said. 'And, if there has never been any sign of these jewels after all this time, there is a possibility they never left the premises on that fateful night.'

'Yes, you are right. Wouldn't it be wonderful if we could find them for Mathilde?' said Ros.

'Yes, and for you, my darling, because if you haven't realised, you are Mathilde's only living relative.'

'But that does not mean any of it will be mine.'

'We shall see.'

They finished their lunch and got up to continue their journey. They had been walking for another fifteen minutes, when they began to notice rocks strewn about the tunnel floor. It became more and more difficult to progress, as there were so many rocks everywhere.

JJ shone the torch ahead of them into the distance. 'Oh no!' he remarked. 'It looks like the tunnel has caved in. There has been a considerable rockfall.'

They carefully picked their way along the tunnel, until it became impossible to go any further. The rockfall had filled the tunnel completely. They both felt very disappointed and downhearted; they had come so far and now it was a dead end. JJ shone the torch over the pile of fallen debris; he could tell it wasn't a recent fall and felt it was stable enough to remove a few stones, to see beyond the cave-in.

'Come on, Ros. Let's move some of these stones. There must be something behind them.'

'Ok. You pass them to me, and I will pile them up along the side of the tunnel.'

They began shifting rocks. None of them were particularly big; it was just that there were a lot of them.

After a while, JJ stopped and shone the torch onto the rocks again. 'I think I can see some sort of open space behind the pile of stones, Rosalinde.'

'Great! Let's keep going.'

An opening was beginning to appear at the top of the pile, about the size of a brick. This spurred them on and, as soon as JJ could get the torch through the hole to look at what was in the space, he did:

It was a sort of room. He presumed it was circular before the rockfall and he could see where the roof had caved in. The air in the room was very cold, but fresh, which surprised him. He couldn't see completely into the room; they needed to remove more stones, so they could get a better view.

They carried on working for another half an hour, carefully removing the rocks. The hole was big enough now for JJ to put his head right in and shine the torch around the whole space. He began to the left, shining the torch along the top of the room, assessing how safe it was, in case of another rockfall. It looked as if the cave-in had happened centuries ago. He felt safe enough to risk leaning further in and, as he did, the beam of the torch caught something unusual.

It was something more jagged and sharp, not like the rocks and stones he had become accustomed to. He took a deep breath inwards, as he shone the torch over what looked like a skeleton.

'Oh my God, Ros! It must be her!' he exclaimed.

'What? What can you see?' she replied, excitedly.

'It's a skeleton. I can only see the top of it, but it must be Sophie, the governess.'

'Oh my God! That is awful. It means she must have died here, in the rockfall.'

'Yes, it certainly looks that way. We have to keep going, Ros. If she's in there, you know what that means.'

'The jewels are there, as well. Oh my God! We have solved the mystery, after all these years.' Rosalinde began to cry. The emotions of the last few days were all becoming too much for her.

JJ climbed down from the rocks to comfort her and hold her in his arms. 'Ros, it's ok. You are safe – I'm here and I'm never going to leave you.'

'I know. It's not that. That poor girl – she must have been terrified.'

'I know. Well, we have found her, and now she can be laid to rest in peace.'

'Yes, that is true.' Rosalinde dried her tears and they continued to remove the stones, until they could both crawl through the hole.

Sophie was sitting up, leaning against the wall. On her lap was a rotten ball of cloth; Rosalinde bent down and gently unfolded it. As soon as she touched it, it disintegrated. Even in the dim light, the jewels dazzled. They both looked at each other in disbelief; they had found the jewels.

Chapter Twenty-Two.

After the remains were identified by DNA to be Sophie, Mathilde's and Rosalinde's ancestor, she was given a Christian burial in the family mausoleum. The authorities were happy that the body was that of Sophie and that the jewels belonged to the La Roche family, and so they were returned to Mathilde at the château.

It had been confirmed by the coroner that Sophie had been hit on the head during the tunnel collapse, causing her to die instantly. This was some comfort to Rosalinde and Mathilde, who worried she might have starved – a slow, agonising death.

The past few weeks had been a complete whirlwind for them all and the shock of finding not only a body, but the family's treasure, which had been missing for over two hundred years, had brought them all to a shuddering halt. There was a lot of media interest in their story, even though they had done their best to keep it quiet. It was like a fairytale, from the terror of Rosalinde's kidnap to finding love with JJ, and finding her grandmother. Now, on top of that, she had found Sophie and the jewels.

They were all completely overwhelmed and had taken themselves off to various parts of the château to come to terms with the latest events. Mathilde was in her boudoir, which, of course, was the grandest bedroom in the château. It had been updated over the years, but still possessed the elegant charm of the original decor. It was a large room; the light poured in through the tall windows on the west side of the house, giving the space a warm glow in the afternoon sunshine. Mathilde was relaxing on a chaise longue in front of a window. She could not believe that, after all these years, the jewels had finally been found. All the excitement had been too much for her and she had had to spend a lot of time reposing in her room. It had given her time to think and come to a few decisions. She hadn't joined the family for dinner for the last few days, preferring a tray in her room. Rosalinde had been popping in to see her, as had Ellen, who had become a firm friend and had been a real help in her recovery. Tonight, she had decided she would go down to dinner, as she had some announcements to make.

Rosalinde had spent the last few days in sheer bliss with JJ; their relationship was growing stronger day by day. Finding Sophie and the jewels had been a massive shock, but it was extremely satisfying to clear up the age-old mystery. Rosalinde's mother, Ellen, really liked JJ, which made her very happy as well. The police had been in touch to say they had gathered forensic evidence from the kidnap scene and were sending Guy Moreau to trial in September. He had pleaded guilty, so with any luck, Rosalinde wouldn't have to give evidence.

There was a knock on the door. Then JJ's head appeared. 'Hi, I wondered if you would like to go for a walk.'

'Yes, I was wondering where you were. I'd love to.'

'Great! Let's go.'

They set off down the grand staircase and out through the front door. At times, Rosalinde kept trying to picture Sophie running down the stairs and out into the gardens after the children, but, of course, she didn't know what she had looked like. She shook her head to clear the fuzzy image and concentrate on what JJ was saying.

'I thought we could walk down to the lake and then on to the woods,' he said excitedly.

'That sounds lovely. I've got my camera – maybe I can take a few shots.'

It was a beautiful afternoon – not a cloud in the sky – as they walked down to the lake. It was so peaceful; the only sound was birdsong.

Rosalinde noticed JJ was carrying a rucksack on his back. 'What have you got in there?' she asked.

'Oh, I brought the rug and something to drink. Maybe we will find a lovely spot to sit and relax for a while.'

'That sounds wonderful! You always think of everything.'

They walked on, admiring the trees and wildflowers. Every now and then, Rosalinde would take a few shots with her camera. At last, they came to a small clearing in the trees. The sun poured down and the trees shimmered in the heat.

'This looks like a perfect spot to relax,' said JJ.

'Yes, it is beautiful.'

JJ carefully took the rug from the rucksack and laid it on the ground. Rosalinde sat down. Then JJ produced two glass flutes from his bag and a bottle of ice-cold Champagne.

'Wow! When you said a drink, I thought you meant a can of Coke or something. You certainly don't do things by halves!'

'Well, I hope we will have cause to celebrate.' With that, he got down on one knee. 'Rosalinde, I know we have known each other for a short time, but I have completely fallen in love with you and I would like to spend the rest of my life with you.'

Rosalinde was blown away; she had no idea he was going to propose.

'Will you marry me?' he asked.

'Oh, JJ! Yes, of course I will! I love you too,' she replied.

She pulled him into her arms and kissed him. For a few minutes they clung to each other, neither willing to break the magic of the moment. Eventually, JJ broke away, popped the cork on the Champagne and poured it into the flutes. Then they lay on the rug, sipping Champagne in utter bliss.

They must have dozed off in the sunshine, because when they woke up, the sun had dropped down and the air was much cooler.

Ros looked at her watch: it was gone seven. 'Oh my goodness!' she exclaimed. 'We should be getting back – it's nearly dinner time. And I can't wait to tell everyone our news.'

'Yes, come on. It won't take long to get back – there is a shortcut through the woods,' chimed a very happy JJ.

They rushed back to the château, washed and changed, and were promptly down in the salon ready for an aperitif.

'Good evening, Rosalinde and JJ,' Mathilde said, as they entered the room.

Didier was handing round drinks and Ellen was already seated on the sofa next to Mathilde.

'Good evening. Have you all had a good day?'

'Yes,' they all replied together.

Rosalinde could hardly contain her excitement, but she waited until everyone had a drink in their hands, including Didier. She and JJ moved to stand in front of the marble fireplace.

'Grandmother, Mum and dearest Didier, we have some news for you...this afternoon, JJ asked me to marry him and I accepted.'

'Well,' said Ellen, 'I am delighted, but I can't say it's a complete surprise. It's obvious you are meant to be together. Congratulations, my darlings!' She got up and ran across the room to kiss them both.

'Yes, I would like to add my congratulations to you both, too,' said Mathilde. 'And whilst we are making announcements, I have one of my own. But before I do, Didier, please could you open the Champagne I asked you to chill?'

Didier, with the help of JJ, opened and served the Champagne.

'Now, so much has happened in the last few weeks. We all know what – so I won't bore you with it again – but it has made me think, and I have made some big decisions about my future and that of the château. Firstly, I would like to say how wonderful it has been to find my granddaughter, and her mother, of course. Secondly, the discovery of the family jewels has been something completely unexpected and yet life-affirming. So tonight, as we are celebrating the engagement of Rosalinde and JJ, I have decided to hand over the château to you both.'

Rosalinde gasped and then burst into tears. Never in her wildest dreams did she think anything like this was going to happen, when she set off for France to photograph a few châteaux. 'Oh, Grandmother...'

'No, I haven't finished yet, Rosalinde. I have had the jewels assessed and have been told their worth, which, quite frankly, is staggering. They have been valued at ten million euros!'

'What?' Rosalinde couldn't believe it.

'Yes, I know – it is unbelievable – but apparently, some of the stones are extremely rare.'

'Wow! That's amazing,' said JJ.

They were all shocked and paused to take a large sip of their Champagne.

'Yes. Now, what I would like to propose is that some of the jewels are sold and the money used to renovate the château. I have very little capital and realise handing over the château will be quite an undertaking. There are, however, some pieces which I feel should remain as family heirlooms.'

Rosalinde crossed the room and flung her arms around her Grandmother. 'Thank you, thank you! I will never be able to thank you enough!'

'It is your birthright. If your father was alive it would have gone to him and then on to you, but as, sadly, he is no longer with us...'

They all raised their glasses to absent friends, thinking of Louis, Rosalinde's father, and, of course, Sophie. Over dinner, they discussed the future and which of the jewels they would like to keep.

'Grandmother, please may I request that we keep the diamond and sapphire necklace that is in the painting?'

'Yes, of course. I was thinking of that one, as it is so prominent in the painting. It goes with the history of the château and it should be kept in the family.'

Mathilde looked around the table at her new family; she felt happier and more content than she had for years. Fate was an unusual thing. Who knew that, when she had agreed to be in the home decoration magazine all those months ago, she would have found her granddaughter, her family's long-lost fortune and security for her remaining years?

Epilogue –1792.

Sophie couldn't hear anything now; she was too far away from the mob to hear them in the tunnel. Thank goodness she had managed to get away in time! She was exhausted and the jewels were very heavy; it had been a long, stressful day. The further she went in the tunnel, the colder it became. She hoped the candle would last until she made it to the ice house. She knew there was a way out of the tunnel in the ice house; she had seen the outside workers pushing the ice down through the doorway. Even if she had to climb out, she would do it, leaving the jewels to be collected later, if necessary.

Sophie hadn't thought about where she would go when she managed to escape from the ice house. For now, it was all about getting away safely.

Above, in the house, the mob had made it to the cellars. As soon as they found the racks upon racks of wine, Champagne, and brandy, they had abandoned any idea of burning down the château. Corks were popped, and they spent the rest of the night drinking and carrying crates and crates of wine up to the kitchen. Someone organized a horse and cart to help carry the wine away. They also raided all the food stores in the cellar. By the time they had finished, most were so drunk that they fell asleep on the cold, stone floor. The cellars of Château La Roche had never seen so much activity and so many pairs of feet up and down the stairs. The original horse and cart had been joined by two more; they were gradually being filled by the jubilant villagers. They had forgotten their intention was to burn the château to the ground, buoyed up with alcohol, and the prospect of a decent meal when they got home, with all the provisions they had gleaned.

The carts were waiting on the west lawn, loaded to the hilt. Dawn was beginning to break, and the birds had started their morning chorus. Finally, the leader of the pack declared the cellars empty. For those who were still conscious, it was time to go home; the rest of them could sleep it off in the cellar.

Far below them, in the tunnel, Sophie was oblivious to everything going on above her. She knew she must be close to the ice house, as it was absolutely freezing. She shivered and wished she had had time to put on warmer clothing. She put down the jewels wrapped in her shawl and rubbed her arms, trying to warm herself. It was no good; she had to keep going. If she stopped now, she would freeze to death.

Sophie thought she could hear something from above. She held the candle up, just in time to see the stones start to shake above her head. She had barely picked up the bundle of jewels, before the whole roof of the tunnel collapsed down onto her. She tried to wriggle free, but a hefty blow to the head killed her instantly. She fell down onto the floor, back to the wall, the bundle on her lap. And that is where she remained for two hundred and twenty years, until Rosalinde and JJ found her.

The End.

Acknowledgements

The idea for this book came when I was holidaying with my family in France several years ago. Whilst driving along a remote country lane, we spotted the most beautiful château through some wrought iron gates. It looked as if it had been lost in time, the silver-grey tiles shimmering in the sunlight. We drove on, but I could not stop thinking about the château. Who lived there? What was it like inside? What stories could it tell?

So, I decided to make up my own story. The château does exist, but all the characters in this story are from my own imagination.

I have had a lot of support from my family and friends during the years it has taken me to write this book, and I would especially like to thank the following people:

- Deb Brown for reading the first draft and giving me her thoughts, which were very helpful, as well as Jason Ayres, writer (and my brother), who encouraged me and helped me with publishing.
- Amy-Louise Armstrong and Chloe Hayes, my daughters, who helped in numerous ways, especially technical support.
- Sarah Hartley for proofreading my novel and correcting my mistakes.
- Lastly, my husband, Paul, who has put up with being dragged around numerous chateaux and has had to listen to my ramblings. Although some of his suggestions were a bit random, I do appreciate that he has supported me through this endeavor.

Printed in Poland
by Amazon Fulfillment
Poland Sp. z o.o., Wrocław